PRAISE FOR
A CHANCE TO CHANGE

"I loved your book. It's so beautifully and powerfully written. Not only is it a great read—just on a story level—it's a great read spiritually. The Lord absolutely spoke to me through your book, and my husband and I have had some conversations because of it. I know this book will bless many, many families. Just such a treat and filled with such goodness."

-   Carla R., editor, mother of three teenagers/young adults, and wife of nearly twenty-seven years

A CHANCE TO CHANGE

Derek and Amy Weichel

To request permissions, contact the publisher at amy@faithfulparent.org

Paperback ISBN: 979-8-9885574-0-1
eBook ISBN: 979-8-9885574-1-8
Audiobook ISBN: 979-8-9885574-2-5

Library of Congress Control Number: 2023911794

First paperback edition: July 2023

Printed in the USA

Faithful Servant, LLC
Beatrice, NE 68310

Faithfulparent.org

ACKNOWLEDGEMENTS

First, we thank God for all the blessings he has showered upon us: eternal life through the life, death, and resurrection of Jesus; His unconditional love so that we can try to model that for our children; the blessing of family; and for the ideas presented in this book that we can now share to try to help others on their parenting journey.

Cole, Leah, Lexi, and Lily, we thank God that He has entrusted you to our care. It is such a joy to watch you grow and learn each day. We love you!

Jennifer, thank you for helping to craft the ideas in this book into a great story and for helping us keep this book focused on Christ. You are truly a gift from God!

Steve, thank you for inspiring, encouraging, and guiding us on this writing journey.

TABLE OF CONTENTS

CHAPTER 1

I t was a lie.

Nicole Richardson sighed, her eyes resting on the framed photo sitting on her kitchen windowsill. The scene was stunning. White sand. Turquoise water. A mariachi band visible in the background under a small canopy of palm trees, shadows dancing across the faces of the musicians. And in the foreground, six faces plastered with forced smiles, smoothies, and umbrella drinks in hand. It was a perfect photo.

But she knew better.

The kitchen timer beeped insistently. Nicole slipped oven mitts over her hands and opened the door. Warm steam smelling of garlic and tomatoes wafted into the air, and she smiled. *Perfect.* She hadn't made lasagna in ages and had been a little nervous that it wasn't going to turn out.

She pulled the casserole dish off the rack and set it on the gray-and-white granite countertop, quickly slipping two loaves of foil-wrapped garlic bread into the oven. Not homemade, but who really baked bread anymore?

Nicole pulled a bag of Caesar salad out of the fridge and looked back at the family photo. It really was beautiful. No one would know that her heart had felt like it was breaking that day, her high hopes for their family vacation having crashed and burned. She had spent months planning their trip to Mexico, counting the days until they were away from work and sports and dance classes, with nothing on their schedule except the anticipation of hours at the beach, swimming, shopping, and playing games. A vacation to connect as a family.

Instead, everyone had scattered. At least, that's what it had felt like. Sam had stayed behind at the hotel to get settled while the rest of them walked down to the beach. Within five minutes of arriving, Tyler had found a group of high schoolers playing sand volleyball and Kyle ran off to boogie board with two boys he'd met on the hotel shuttle. And the girls....

Nicole opened the bags of salad and dumped them in a bowl, frustration flaring at the memory. Abby was usually the one who took the brunt of Hannah's moods, and that day had been no different. Abby had asked Hannah to play in the ocean with her, but Hannah had flopped dramatically onto her towel and refused. Nicole remembered the disappointment in her youngest daughter's eyes as she sighed and wandered away to build a sandcastle by herself.

"Hannah, she wants to be with you. And she can't go in the ocean alone, you know that."

"Then *you* go."

Nicole had bitten back a retort. "I am planning to go, but she wants to spend time with you."

Hannah had rolled her eyes, her dark blonde ponytail swinging from side to side. "I sat with her on the plane. I'm done babysitting." She raised her eyebrows. "Maybe if I had my *phone,* I'd want to go take pictures. But *someone* said I had to leave it at the hotel."

Ah, yes. That was it. Hannah was mad at the world because her precious phone was elsewhere.

Nicole dressed the salad and tossed it, sprinkling croutons on top. The rest of the vacation had been more of the same. Hannah had eventually come around and apologized for her attitude, but still had run off with girls her own age whenever she could. When they were back at their hotel, phones and tablets were the chosen activities rather than the board games she'd imagined. Sam kept stepping away to take conference calls and answer questions from clients, and Nicole had found herself staring at her family, all together in one room and yet worlds apart. How had it gotten like this?

She set six plates at the table and doled out silverware at each setting. Tonight would be different. School had been in session for almost two months, and they were all so busy: Kyle was in football, the girls had dance, and Tyler hadn't been home since his college courses started six weeks ago. Add to that Sam's work schedule and overtime, her own side business, and shuttling everyone to various events, Nicole felt that they were busier and further apart than they'd ever been before. She'd had enough.

Tonight would be the start of something different.

Twenty years with Sam as of today. She felt herself smile. Her one request had been that everyone be home for a family dinner together. It had been so long since they'd all been in one place sharing a meal, and tonight had been the only one available in the past two weeks. She mentally went over the evening's plans in her head. *Sam home at 5:00 to make dessert with me. Kids home at 5:15. Dinner at 5:30. Kids leave for the church event at 6:30. Tyler spends the evening with Mason. Everyone home by ten.* And in the meantime, she and Sam would have a chance to relax together with a bottle of wine on the back porch like they used to when they were newly married. Except back then it had been a cheap glass of boxed wine on the tiny balcony outside their second-floor apartment.

She set the final fork next to Sam's plate. He would love that she made lasagna. It had always been his favorite. If she were honest, she was hoping tonight would be a chance for the two of them to reconnect and have the closeness she remembered during their early years. That's one reason she'd made the lasagna and planned the evening on the porch: It's what they'd done on their very first anniversary. Back when they'd been living paycheck to paycheck, when an unexpected car repair meant dipping into their measly three-hundred-dollar savings account and eating Top Ramen for lunch the next week. Without any room in the budget for a night out, instead of dinner and a movie in the city, she'd made lasagna and he'd splurged on a single rose and the cheapest box of wine he could find. The two of them had spent the evening talking, ultimately pulling their wedding cake out of the freezer and laughing hysterically at how bad it tasted after a year next to the frozen chicken. All their future dreams burned bright, unfulfilled ahead of them. So simple. So sweet. So unlike her life now.

She glanced at the clock. It was 5:08. She frowned and checked her phone. No texts from Sam, but there was one from Tyler. Her thumb tapped the screen and a speech bubble popped into view. *Hey Mom, I'm not going to be able to make it after all. Sorry, hope you have a good night.* Nicole felt her heart drop and fought a wave of panic. Maybe if he knew they wanted him home—that *she* wanted him home—but no, she didn't want to push him away. Didn't want to smother him when he was out on his own for the first time. Her fingers trembled over the buttons. *Are you okay? Are you sure? We are so excited to see you, honey.* She pushed send, silently praying that her small nudge might make him change his mind.

Minutes ticked by. She fought the urge to text Sam and ask where he was, knowing that doing so would only irritate him. They were supposed to make dessert together, and she wasn't sure if she should start without him or wait. She checked her phone for the fifth time in as many minutes, then heard the front door slam and three pairs of feet come traipsing through the entry as Hannah yelled, "Thanks, Mrs. Schanaman!"

"What *smells* so good?" Abby asked, walking through the living room and dropping her backpack unceremoniously onto the couch. "I know I like it, but I can't remember what it is."

"Lasagna," Nicole answered, her phone screen still stubbornly blank. She forced a smile and wrapped her arms around her youngest. "How was school? And dance?"

Abby slid onto a barstool, auburn curls bouncing. "It was good! I aced my spelling test, and Mrs. Jasper said she wants me to do a solo in the winter recital." She wrinkled her nose. "But we started multiplication in math, and I suck at it."

"You don't suck at it. You're learning. There's a difference," Nicole corrected, then winced. "And don't say 'suck.'"

Her phone lit up and she scooped it off the counter. Tyler had finally replied. *I'm fine, just busy. Cya.* Nicole's stomach twisted.

"Mom?" Abby asked. "Are you okay?"

"I'm fine," Nicole lied. "Just disappointed. Tyler can't make it tonight."

"Oh." Abby twisted a curl around her finger. "Is he still coming tomorrow? For the weekend, like he said?"

Nicole sighed. "I don't think so, sweetie."

"Tyler isn't coming?" Kyle poked his head into the kitchen, grass stains and dirt streaks visible on his football uniform. "Golden Boy have something better to do?"

Nicole forced a laugh and said, "He's just busy. You will be too when it's your turn for college. We have to be flexible." She nodded in Kyle's direction. "Shower fast, we're supposed to eat in fifteen minutes."

"Will do."

Nicole pulled the bread and lasagna out of the oven. The foil would keep them warm for the last ten minutes or so. *As long as Sam is home by 5:30.*

Abby and Hannah went upstairs to change out of their dance outfits, and Nicole sat staring at the grandfather clock next to the picture window in the living room. The minutes ticked by. Nicole couldn't shake the pit in her stomach. Half an hour passed without a word from Sam. Finally at 5:45, she decided she'd risk his annoyance and text him. *He's forty-five minutes later than he said and fifteen minutes late for dinner. If anyone has a right to be annoyed, it's me. Not him*, she thought. She punched the keys and hit send. *Everything okay? We're ready to eat.* She slipped the foil-covered meal back into the oven to keep warm and tried to push the frustration bubbling inside her down deep.

Tick, tick, tick. The clock was taunting her, pointing out every second Sam failed to deliver his presence on their special night. Her phone remained silent. *I am not making dessert alone. If he wants to be this late without calling, he can have it tomorrow and make it himself.* Nicole clenched her jaw and started to pace. A normal wife would probably be frantic by now, but she'd been stood up by Sam enough times to jump straight to anger. Sure, sometimes he took overtime without telling her, she just didn't think he'd do it *tonight*.

Dong! Dong! Dong! Dong! Dong! Dong!

The clock's chimes died away and Hannah walked into the kitchen dressed in blue jeans and a purple sweater. "Mom?" She looked at Nicole's face and hesitated. "Um, Kara's mom wants to know if she can pick us up ten minutes early because she has an extra errand she needs to run."

Nicole pinched the bridge of her nose and squeezed her eyes shut. "That's fine. Can you tell Kyle and Abby to please come and eat?"

"Sure." Hannah bit her lip, a worry line forming between her eyebrows. "I'm really sorry Dad isn't here yet."

Nicole sighed. "Me too." *Not as sorry as he's going to be.*

As Hannah ran upstairs, Nicole pulled the lasagna and bread out of the oven and set them on the counter. She'd planned to light candles on the table, use cloth napkins, and savor the meal with Sam and the kids. But now, what was the point? She set up a buffet line on the island—lasagna, salad, dressings, bread, and butter—and scooped four plates off the table. She set three in a stack next to the lasagna and gently placed the fourth—Tyler's—back in the cupboard. She could hear feet pounding on the stairs as she sank onto one of the bar stools. So much for her family dinner.

The kids ate quickly, hours of her hard work disappearing in a rush so that they'd be ready to leave on time. The girls ate at the table while Kyle stood at the counter, dark hair wet from his shower. He was still scooping up lasagna sauce with his bread when a car honked outside.

"Bye, Mom! Love you!" Hannah plopped her dish in the sink, gave Nicole a quick hug, and ran to grab her coat and sneakers from the entryway. Kyle snagged two more pieces of bread and followed her, waving over his shoulder with his mouth full. Only Abby stayed behind, her small form slumped in the dining chair.

"I don't wanna go."

Nicole raised her eyebrows, and she slid off the bar stool. "What? Why not?"

Abby leaned forward and rested her chin next to her plate. "I'm tired. I just want to be home with you and Daddy."

"Well, Daddy isn't home." The words came out harsher than she'd anticipated, and Nicole could hear how bitter they sounded. She pulled the empty chair next to Abby away from the table and sat down. She forced her voice to soften. "I mean, he's not home yet."

Abby tilted her head. "I know. I guess I could just be home with you."

Nicole felt a smile tug at her lips. *My sweet girl.* "I think you should go to the Harvest Festival. You've been looking forward to it for a month."

Abby sighed. "Yeah, but I didn't know I'd be this tired. I'd rather just watch a movie and stay home."

The door opened and Kyle's voice boomed from the entry. "Abby, we have to go! Get out here!"

Nicole ran a hand through her daughter's curls. "I think you'll be sad if you miss it, and Mrs. Wellum is waiting. Let's go." Abby moaned, and Nicole laughed as she squeezed her shoulders. "Come on, kiddo."

Abby laced up her boots at the front door and slid her arms into her coat. Nicole kissed her cheek and gave her a big squeeze. "Have a blast, okay?"

Abby nodded, curls bouncing. "I will, but I'm sleeping in tomorrow."

"Deal." Nicole shooed her out the door and watched her climb into the van next to Kyle. "Thanks, Heather!" Nicole called, waving from the porch as they pulled away from the curb, headlights flashing in the quickly dimming evening night. *Have fun.*

Nicole stepped back inside the now-quiet house. It was almost 6:30. She walked into the kitchen, and her eyes surveyed the counter. The lasagna was getting cold and already half gone, the salad's lettuce was limp, and only a third of the bread remained, largely thanks to Kyle.

Angry tears pricked her eyes, but she refused to let them fall. Of all the ways this evening could have gone, this was one she'd never anticipated. *But I should have.* Sam had stood her up before. If she was honest, this wasn't an irregular thing. Stuff always seemed to "come up" with him, and she was often the last to know. But she'd assumed that if something were really and truly important, that he'd remember and make it a priority.

She'd been wrong.

Nicole picked up Abby's plate and placed it in the sink. She turned on the faucet and grabbed a dishrag, beginning to scrub away the remainders of sauce and cheese. Enough was enough. Something had to change.

And that something was Sam.

***

Sam Richardson pulled his truck into the garage and pressed the button attached to his sun visor with a sigh. He was finally home. *What a day.* He hated getting home after seven, but the side job he'd picked up after work had been too promising. It had been the right call. The payout on this job would be bigger than he'd originally hoped and would definitely help with the extra money they needed to cover Tyler's college. Sam grabbed the empty fast-food bag in the passenger seat to throw away. McDonald's for dinner wasn't ideal, but at least now Nicole didn't need to worry about making him something. Sam stepped out of his truck and crossed to the garage entry door. He was so glad to be home.

The smell of garlic, sausage, and onion accosted him the second he entered the house, and he knew he'd blown it.

Lasagna sat half-eaten on the kitchen island, and Sam swore quietly under his breath. How in the world had he forgotten? He frantically looked at his watch. The digital time blared accusingly at him: *7:15.* He closed his eyes, a sinking feeling in his stomach. Nicole would never forgive him.

"Looks like you finally remembered where we live." Nicole sat at the dining table, empty plate in front of her, a glass of wine half full in her hand.

"Ahhh..."

"Excellent use of English, Sam."

Irritation flared, and Sam squeezed the incriminating McDonald's bag, sorely wishing he'd left it in the truck. "I know you're mad, but let's not do this, please."

Nicole's eyes flashed. "Do what? Talk about how you missed our twentieth anniversary that we planned together? Or how I made the effort to make your favorite meal? Or maybe how I didn't make dessert because you never showed up to make it with me? Yeah, let's not. Maybe instead we should talk about how you never returned my texts. Or how you didn't see the kids at all today. *Again.*"

Sam shoved the McDonald's bag into the standing trash can and crossed his arms, any shred of guilty feelings quickly fading at the look on his wife's face. A muscle jerked in his jaw. "Look, I'm sorry I missed it, and yes, I did forget. But I had other things that came up that needed my attention, and I need you to trust me on this."

Nicole let out a cynical laugh. "I'm supposed to trust you that something at work came up that was more important than our anniversary? Ouch." She took a sip of wine. "You're an electrician, Sam. Unless something literally caught on fire, I doubt it was that important."

Sam tugged off his jacket and flung it over a dining chair. "I don't have to justify every decision I make to you. I said I was sorry. What else do you want me to do?"

Nicole set down her wine glass too hard, red liquid sloshing onto the white tablecloth. "How about actually being sorry? You say the words, Sam. And then you do it again."

"I've never missed an anniversary!"

"That's not the point!"

Sam rubbed his hands over his face. "Be reasonable, please. I've had a very long day."

Something about the way his voice cracked must have indicated that something was wrong because Nicole was silent for a moment. Then, in a low voice she asked, "What happened?"

Sam rested his hands on the back of the dining chair. "Did Tyler call you?"

"He texted me. Said he couldn't make it for dinner."

Sam winced. The pain in her voice was unmistakable, and he wanted to shake his son. "I told him to call."

Nicole let out a broken laugh. "Please tell me the irony of that comment is not lost on you."

Sam held up his hands in surrender. "All right, fine. Yes. I get it. The Richardson men are terrible at phones today." He took a deep breath and blew it out. "Tyler's in some trouble."

Sam watched his wife's anger turn rapidly into alarm. "What kind of trouble? How do you know?"

"He called me at work." Sam drummed his fingers on the back of the chair. "Apparently last night, he went out to a party with some friends. The cops showed up, and he got a ticket."

"For what?"

Sam paused and looked at her. He wasn't supposed to be the one to break this news and he felt his anger at Tyler rise. "Minor in possession of alcohol."

Nicole stared at him. "But Tyler doesn't drink."

For heaven's sake, she could be so naïve. "Apparently, he does."

Nicole sat back in her chair and closed her eyes. "We prepped him for this. We talked to him before he left about this stuff. What on earth is he thinking?"

Sam grunted and pulled out the chair. "He isn't. But that's not his only problem." He sank into it, the heaviness in the air settling like a wet blanket. "He also just got notice that his scholarship is in jeopardy."

"Why?"

"Evidently, this wasn't his first party. It's become somewhat of a habit, and his grades are tanking. He goes to class, goes to work, and goes to parties. Homework hasn't been a priority." Sam crossed his arms and sighed. "Honestly, I don't think we'd know about any of this if he hadn't gotten the ticket. I could tell it really shook him up."

A tear trickled steadily down one of Nicole's cheeks. "And he wouldn't tell me about it."

Sam shook his head. "I don't think he wanted to disappoint you."

"Has he been going to Leanne's church?" Nicole wiped her eyes in frustration. "I talked to her two weeks ago, and she said she has only seen him there once since school started, but I just thought maybe they attended different services."

"I doubt he's been, by the sound of it," Sam replied. He stretched his neck from side to side, a tension headache forming. "From what I can tell, we're paying thousands of dollars so our son can make stupid choices with his friends."

"Oh my word, Sam! Why is it always about money with you?" Nicole angrily pushed back her chair and snatched her glass from the table. "This is our son's life, and all you can think about is our finances?"

Sam rolled his eyes. "Of course not. I'm obviously worried about Tyler, but I also have zero interest in paying that school a bunch of money if he's going to waste it on partying. We're paying for his education, not a booze cruise." He ran a hand through his hair, exhaustion rolling over him like a wave. "I'm not picking up all these extra side jobs just so he can drink them."

Nicole swirled water around in her glass and set it in the sink, her voice cold. "Well, to me it sounds like you're more upset about how much money you're out than you are about our son jeopardizing his future."

Sam let out a frustrated bark. "Will you stop it? The money isn't the point, but let's not pretend it isn't a factor here."

"I don't care about the money!"

"You never do!" Sam surged to his feet, his voice raised. "You think that Tyler's tuition is the only reason I'm taking side jobs? What about you and your choices? Your trips to the spa. Eating out with your friends. Shopping with the girls." He shook his head. "You want a certain kind of lifestyle, but if I miss dinner for work, you've got me pegged as some sort of self-centered jerk!" He was yelling now. If he didn't leave the room, he knew he'd regret it.

Nicole whirled to face him, eyes blazing. "It wasn't just dinner, and you know it. It's our twentieth anniversary, and you literally couldn't be bothered to show up!"

"I apologized!"

"And then told me it was my fault for going to the spa?" Nicole shook her head incredulously. "And Tyler's fault for going to college?"

Sam walked to the fridge and jerked open the door. He reached inside and grabbed a microbrew. "That's not what I said, and you know it."

But Nicole was beside herself. Angry tears were back in her eyes. "Our family is a wreck."

Sam slammed the fridge door shut. "Stop being so dramatic!"

Nicole glared at him. "Our son is about to lose his scholarship, you forgot our anniversary, and I'm the only one who seems to think this is a sign of an actual problem."

Sam walked over to the door to the basement. "Stuff happens, Nicole. People aren't perfect. Not having enough to eat? Foreclosing the house? Having cancer? Those are *actual* problems." Did she have any idea how good they had it? "I'm done with this conversation. Sorry I ruined your night."

He could hear the sarcasm in his voice and knew she did too. The last thing he heard as he descended the basement stairs was her angry reply of, "Sure you are," and the slam of the door.

CHAPTER 2

"**M**om, where are my ballet slippers?!"

The panicked cry was a more effective alarm clock than Nicole could have set herself, and she moaned under her breath, rolling over in bed. She slowly opened her eyes and winced. Her eyelids were puffy and stiff, a souvenir from her tears of the night before. *Lovely.*

"Mooooooom!" Hannah burst into the room, her ballet costume half-hanging off her shoulder. "I can't find my slippers! I know I put them in my backpack, but they aren't there!"

Nicole rubbed her eyes. "Did you check the inside pocket? You know sometimes they accidentally slip into it."

Hannah bounced on the balls of her feet, voice turning shrill. "I did, and they aren't there! And if I can't find them, *how* am I supposed to dance today?"

The dance recital. This morning. Right.

Nicole sat up and sighed. "You have a backup pair of shoes for this exact reason, but you also still have time to search. Are you sure you had them in your bag yesterday?"

"YES!"

"And you didn't take them out?"

"NO!"

"Hannah, please." Nicole could feel a headache coming on. "I'm sitting a few feet away from you, you don't need to shriek. We'll find the shoes or use the spares. It's fine."

Hannah growled and turned on her heel. Nicole could hear her stalking down the hallway. The shoes were probably still in her dance bag, and she just hadn't looked hard enough.

Nicole pushed back the blankets and swung her legs off the side of her bed, searching with her feet for her slippers. She pulled the sheets and comforter up to the head of the bed and paused. Sam's side of the bed was smooth. Too smooth, which meant he hadn't come to bed last night and she'd slept in their room alone. He must have slept in the recliner in the man-cave downstairs.

Again.

Her stomach dropped. This was becoming less of an anomaly and more of a pattern as of late. Something would set one of them off, they would fight, and rather than come to bed and be with her, he'd stay away. *It's like I'm not even worth fighting for.* Nicole picked up three throw pillows and arranged them on the bed. *Then again, he didn't show up for our anniversary dinner, so I guess he's consistent.*

Sunlight streamed through the windows onto the hardwood floor. Nicole made her way to the bathroom, irritation at Sam making her frown. She cringed as she glanced at the mirror and stepped closer to inspect her reflection.

She was a disaster. Her eyes were red-rimmed and swollen, and... were those shadows forming underneath? Dark hair hung limp around her face, except for one wild section sticking up in the back as if it were doing some crazy salute. Her skin was equal parts blotchy and pale, and she could see a pimple forming on the end of her nose. Now, that was just unfair. No one should have to deal with acne after forty.

Nicole shook her head to clear it and pulled her tee shirt over her head. She and Sam needed to talk. She knew it meant they'd also probably end up in another giant fight, but it was a fight that needed to happen—one that couldn't end with him running away to the basement while she spent another night alone in their bed. Nicole slid open the glass shower door and twisted the faucet handle to its highest setting. She was willing to fight this out. She needed to tell him that.

She stepped into the shower. Hopefully the heat would wash away the swelling, and whatever remained makeup could cover. Mascara could do wonders for swollen eyes, and if she still needed to look more alert after that, there was always coffee.

* * *

The dance recital was scheduled for 10:00 and it was only 9:10. Nicole closed her bedroom door and walked briskly down the hall, drawing a brush through her hair as she went. If the kids had already eaten, maybe she and Sam could talk before she had to leave with the girls. The dance studio was only ten minutes away, and they needed to be there a few minutes early, but this meant she could probably count on a good thirty minutes of conversation before everyone had to grab coats and shoes and run out the door.

Hannah was standing at the kitchen table, rifling through her dance bag. "They aren't here, and I've looked four times!"

Nicole lifted a coffee mug down from the cabinet and reached for the coffee pot. "Your spares are in my closet, but don't worry. I'll help you look in just a minute." Nicole took a sip. Too bitter. She wanted creamer this morning. "Where's your dad?"

Hannah zipped up her bag and collapsed into a dining chair with a "humph." She fiddled with the name tag hanging from the side. "He left already. He said he had to check on a job before the golf tournament later."

"Oh, I totally forgot about that tournament." Nicole poured hazelnut creamer into her coffee mug, disappointed. Not that she was involved in any capacity, but Sam had told her last week that he expected it to go all afternoon and into the evening. If he was gone already and she was leaving in less than an hour, they wouldn't be crossing paths until tonight. So much for getting to the bottom of their marital issues.

She sat down next to Hannah and took a drink of her now-sweet mug of coffee. "Where's Kyle?"

Hannah raised her eyebrows. "Mom, he's at Judah's, remember? He called you last night and asked if he could stay over?"

"Oh. Right."

A half-smile formed at the side of Hannah's mouth. "Hi, I'm Hannah. I'm your daughter. Your name is Nicole. You know, in case you forgot that stuff too."

"Haha." Nicole smiled and shook her head. "I'm apparently really out of it today."

Hannah wiggled her eyebrows. "I'm sixteen, and you let me drive whenever I want."

This time, Nicole laughed. "Nice try." She wrapped both hands around her cup, savoring the warmth sinking into her skin. "Is Abby ready to go? The three of us could probably search together."

"I haven't seen her." Hannah reached towards the mug. "Can I have the end?"

"Like you need coffee." Nicole pulled the cup away from Hannah and stood up. "Come on. I'll drink. You lead. We'll both search."

Hannah jumped up from her chair and led the way out of the kitchen, through the hallway, and up the staircase. "Mom, seriously, I've looked everywhere."

"Two pairs of eyes are better than one. And three is better than two." They reached the top of the stairs and turned right down the corridor that led to the girls' rooms and the entrance to the attic over the garage. She reached Abby's door and knocked with her knuckles before twisting the door handle. "Abs? You ready to go? We need help finding Hannah's slippers."

Nicole opened the door to find Abby kneeling in the middle of her room, frantically digging through her own dance bag. She was tousle-haired, sleepy-eyed, still in rumpled pajamas, and had very obviously only been awake for approximately ninety seconds.

"ABBY!" Hannah's shriek echoed off the walls, and her younger sister winced. "We have to go in half an hour!"

"Don't yell at me!" Abby's lower lip trembled, and she rubbed her eyes. "I slept in. I was so tired. I'll be ready."

Hannah let out a frustrated yelp, pushing past Nicole and grabbing something off the floor. "*You* had my slippers?!" She glared at her sister, fury on her face. "I've been looking for these all morning, dummy! And you stole them!"

"Hannah, that's enough!" Abby burst into tears and Nicole pulled her into her arms. "You may not call her names. Apologize!"

Hannah's eyes sparked. "Well, it was dumb of her to steal my slippers so that name fits!"

"*Stop it!*" Did the meanness of twelve-year-olds know no bounds? "You don't know why she had them. You might have accidentally put them in her bag."

Hannah glared at Abby. "That's something a dummy would do, not me."

Abby let out a wail. "I was cleaning them! I wanted them to be ready for the recital!" She pointed at the pile of wipes in the trash can. "I was going to give them to you this morning as a surprise, so you didn't have to do it."

Hannah blinked.

Nicole glared at her daughter. "She was trying to do something nice for you."

Hannah looked at Abby, a shadow of shame passing over her face for a moment—and then it was gone. "Don't take my stuff," Hannah said in a low voice, clutching her slippers as she ran out of the room.

Nicole hugged Abby, compassion for her youngest welling up inside her. "That was a very sweet thing you did for your sister. I'm sorry she didn't appreciate it." She glanced at her watch and grimaced. "Honey, I'm so sorry but we are going to be seriously cutting it close if we don't get moving. Can you change into your costume while I pack your dance bag?"

Abby nodded and pulled away, wiping her eyes. "Can you bring my pink unicorn shirt?"

Sweet girl. "Of course."

Thirty minutes later, they were pulling out of the driveway. Ballerina buns were hair-sprayed, small amounts of makeup had been applied, and the dance bags were packed. Nicole glanced in her rearview mirror at the girls. Hannah was glued to her phone, texting madly. Abby was watching YouTube on her tablet, a pile of snacks in her lap to be eaten as a make-shift breakfast on the way to the recital. She was halfway through a granola bar, with a package of chips and two fruit snacks on standby. Breakfast of champions fail.

A sadness Nicole couldn't pinpoint washed over her. She punched the visor button with her thumb and closed the garage door. She put the SUV into drive and sped down the street.

* * *

The Christmas Cheer charity golf tournament was a staple of the Devon Falls community each autumn, but this was the first time Sam had gotten the chance to attend. He whistled under his breath. Food trucks lined the parking lot in a long train of options. He looked at the punch card in his hand. According to the woman who checked his registration, it got him a free meal from any of the trucks, golf for the afternoon, and access to the dinner buffet in the evening. His boss had given him one of the sought-after tickets for being Employee of the Month in September. Overtime was paying off in more ways than one.

Nicole's face flashed through his mind. The benefits were evidently not without consequences.

Picnic tables dotted the grassy field adjacent to the parking lot, already half-filled with participants eating off paper plates and plastic bowls. Sam skimmed the signs of the food trucks before making what he considered an easy decision and moved to stand in line for barbecued brisket.

Two teenagers stood in front of him, one in a baseball cap and the other in a letterman's jacket. If he had to guess, they were probably a year older than Kyle. The school name on the back of the coat was one he recognized but couldn't place. Maybe they were a rival private school Tyler had played in football.

Sam smirked. If Tyler had played against their school, they'd know who he was. Pride swelled in his chest as he thought of his oldest son. Touchdown Tyler: That was the name the local press had given him, and he had lived up to it in spades. He'd been a wide receiver since his sophomore year and only gotten better, leading their relatively unknown high school to the state playoffs three years in a row. By the time he graduated, he'd been the team's undeniable star. Sam had gone to every home game he could, and while he hadn't had perfect attendance, he'd made more than he'd missed. He felt his smile fade and the warmth in his chest cooled. Tyler was too talented to be so stupid with alcohol.

The line moved slowly forward, and Sam checked his watch. He was good on time, but he felt out of place standing alone. Most people seemed to have come with a partner or two. He reached in his back pocket for his phone and clicked the button on the side. A photo of Tyler in full football gear lit up the screen, his smile wide and confident after his final senior game. Sam gently stroked his thumb over his son's face. He missed him.

He missed watching him play too. Kyle was on the team now, but it wasn't the same. A hamstring strain early in the season had caused the coach to slash his play time. And if Sam was honest, Kyle wasn't the star that Tyler was. He was a solid player, and Sam was proud of him for making varsity, but sitting in the stands and hoping his younger son was put on the field wasn't nearly as gratifying as watching his oldest sprint headlong into the endzone.

Not that he'd been to many games this year. Between Kyle's injury and picking up so much overtime, attending was lower on his priority list.

Sam reached the head of the line and ordered, his stomach rumbling as the food-truck attendant handed him a paper box with a huge brisket sandwich covered in sauce and steak fries along with a large soda. It looked incredible. He grabbed a small handful of napkins and made his way to an empty picnic table, balancing the box in his right hand while taking a deep gulp from the Styrofoam cup in his left. Coke hit the spot every time.

"Sam?"

He choked in surprise, soda burning his throat. He coughed and wiped his mouth, looking around for whoever had said his name. Hopefully he hadn't sprayed Coke everywhere.

A man about his age was smiling at him, looking familiar in a generic sort of way. He was probably an old client. He cleared his throat and flashed a smile. "Hi. Can I help you?"

"Tom Miller," the man said, reaching out his hand.

Sam grasped it and shook. The name didn't ring any bells, but then again, it wasn't exactly unique. "You'll have to forgive me. I'm trying to remember how we know each other. Did I do some work for you?"

Tom laughed. "No, nothing like that. Gosh, it's been years since we've seen each other. My oldest son played sports with yours a while back. Tyler, right?"

"That's right." Sam was grasping. He was usually pretty good with faces, but he did meet a lot of people, and apparently Tom hadn't made enough of an impression for instant recall. "Was this in high school?"

"Oh, no. Pretty sure the last time our boys played together was Wyatt's eighth grade year. I think Tyler was a year behind him, so it really was a while ago."

Wyatt. Now that was familiar. There had been a Wyatt on Tyler's baseball team in middle school who had been an excellent player. Tyler had really looked up to him. A distant memory of the Millers began to form in his mind. He was pretty sure they had another kid. Maybe a daughter? "Did he play through Heritage Christian School?"

Tom nodded, brown eyes smiling. "That's him." He held up his left hand, which was filled with his own box of brisket. "Mind if we sit with you? I think you're actually in our golf foursome."

"Am I? All they gave me was a group number."

"I checked the list when we came in," Tom settled onto the bench across from Sam and picked up a fry. "Are you part of Group 18?"

Sam pulled his ticket out of his jacket pocket. "Looks that way." *Good. Better to be with an acquaintance than three perfect strangers.*

"Jess!" Tom waved his hand at a blonde woman who was standing with a young man who resembled her so much, it had to be her son. They each held plates of tacos. "Over here, I found our missing piece." The woman started their way, and Tom motioned with his head. "You probably don't remember my wife. This is Jessica." The younger man sat next to his mother as Sam shook her hand. "And this is Wyatt."

Wyatt grinned and shook Sam's hand. "Nice to meet you."

"Actually, apparently, we've met. You played baseball with my son Tyler several years ago at Heritage."

"Tyler Richardson? Cool. I remember him." Wyatt picked up a taco and took a bite. He grimaced. "I should have gone with brisket."

His mother laughed. "Or just not gotten fish tacos from a truck. Beef is safer." Jessica tore the corner off a packet of hot sauce and squeezed it over her food. She smiled at Sam. "Is Tyler still playing baseball?"

Sam shook his head. "He played his freshman year, but that was it. Football became the sport he was really good at, so he chose the rest of his sports based upon how well they'd keep him conditioned. He played basketball in the winters and ran track in the spring." He swirled a fry into a small cup of ketchup. "He's quite the athlete. Won MVP at Heritage two years in a row."

Tom was already halfway through his own sandwich. "That's awesome! Good for him." He wiped his mouth with a napkin. "So is Tyler in college now? Still playing?"

"He's a freshman at Western and loving it," Sam replied. "He's redshirted this year, so he's practicing with the team but not playing. It's a big school, and as good as he is, they have some really talented upperclassmen." He motioned to Tom. "But how about you? Do you still have kids at Heritage? Or did you move your kids to public for high school?"

Heritage Christian wasn't a tiny school, but it was still small enough that he was somewhat familiar with most of the families who attended. If he hadn't seen Tom and his family for over five years, it was probably because they'd left. AP courses and a desire to get their kids' feet wet outside the Christian bubble was a decision a lot of parents at Heritage made. Plus, high school tuition prices could be a beast if you had more than one child.

Jessica shook her head. "No, we started homeschooling when Wyatt hit high school."

"Seriously?" The question escaped him before he had a chance to consider that they might find his incredulity offensive.

To his relief, all three Millers laughed. Tom picked up his soda and pointed the straw at Sam. "We get that a lot."

"Okay, wait." Sam paused, racking his brain for information. "Wyatt's not your only child, right? Don't you have a daughter?"

"A daughter and a son. Whitney is sixteen and Will just turned thirteen."

A memory, clear this time, rang in Sam's mind. "Wait. Ohhhhh. Will Miller is your son too?"

Tom nodded and Sam laughed. "Will and my daughter Hannah were close buddies in early elementary school. I hadn't put it together that he was Wyatt's brother." Hannah had talked nonstop about her friends at that age, and Will's name was usually at the top of the list.

"Oh, that's right! I forgot about that." Jessica smiled. "And you have another son in between Tyler and Hannah, right? I thought he was near Whitney's age."

"Kyle. He's fifteen and a sophomore at Heritage this year. And then our youngest is Abby, who's eight, but you probably don't know her since she wasn't at Heritage until after you left."

"Oh, eight is a fun age." Jessica elbowed Wyatt. "I miss you at eight."

"Thanks, Mom. The love is palpable." Wyatt finished his taco and stood up to take his garbage to the trash. "Anyone else finished? I can take your stuff."

"No one else inhales food like a vacuum, so no," Tom said.

Wyatt gave a small bow. "You wish you had such talent." He pointed to a group of college students sitting three tables away. "Jackson and Isaac are over there. I'll be back." He held up a hand in a wave at Sam. "Looking forward to golfing with you, Mr. Richardson. Good to see you!"

Sam watched Wyatt jog over to the trash can and then set off to see his friends. "It's obvious you guys have raised a good kid."

"God is kind," Tom said, his eyes following his son. "It's a special kind of blessing to enjoy your kids as people and friends." He leaned back and stretched, lifting his cap off his head and revealing a head full of dark hair peppered lightly with gray. "He's been so busy lately that he hasn't had a lot of social time. I'm glad he found some friends to catch up with."

Sam realized that he hadn't even asked about Wyatt's college, and he mentally kicked himself. "Where's he going to school?"

"He's at the community college here in town, just part-time. But he's working full-time and volunteering with the youth group at church, so his load is pretty heavy." Tom took a final bite of his sandwich and washed it down, then glanced at his watch. "We'd better get our clubs. Our group is scheduled to tee off in about twenty minutes, and we should probably hit the driving range first to warm up."

Jessica dropped the final third of a taco onto her plate. "I'm full anyway." She stood up from the table and wiped it down with a napkin.

Tom rolled his eyes. "You didn't even make a mess."

"Old habits." Jessica took Tom's now-empty paper box and looked at Sam. "We're parked a ways out so it will be a few minutes. Should we meet back here?"

Sam stood up and swung his leg over the picnic table bench. "Actually, how about I go with you and carry Wyatt's clubs? I'm close." He pointed to his truck parked near the course entrance. "I'll just grab mine on the way back."

"Oh! That'd be great. That way Tom doesn't have to do double-duty."

Tom quirked an eyebrow as the three of them started walking. "What are you talking about? I was going to make you carry them." He turned to Sam in explanation. "After twenty-two years of marriage, I found out my wife has been holding out on me."

Jessica laughed and made a face at her husband. "I should have never carried that log. I've given up my secret. Here, take these. There's a trash can right there." Tom took their plates from his wife and tossed them as they passed by. "Okay, I'll explain. So, this spring, we took a family trip to Indonesia."

Sam looked at her in surprise. "What's in Indonesia?"

Tom jumped in to elaborate. "Oh, nothing specific. We do trips like this every year or so as a family. Have you heard of Hands of Mercy?"

Sam shook his head.

"They're a ministry that focuses on missions work overseas that families can go and do together," Tom explained. "Our last trip was to Indonesia. Anyway—" Tom paused to fish his keys out of his pocket. "So we're up in these jungle villages that are extremely remote doing little Bible camps with kids and building projects with the men. Jessica and Whitney were helping lead a VBS for the village kids, and I was doing some construction on a school building with the boys." He clicked the key fab and an older model SUV blinked its headlights. "I'm having Wyatt hold a board for me to keep it straight, and all the guys around me start laughing and pointing and tapping me on the shoulder. I don't speak Indonesian, so I have no idea what's going on, but finally I realize that Jessica is literally hauling a log over to the kids by herself."

Jessica shrugged. "We were doing Noah's ark. I wanted a visual."

Sam laughed. "How big was this log?"

"Honestly, not that big."

"Ha!" Tom barked in protest. "It was pretty big." He popped the trunk of the SUV and reached for a purple bag of clubs. "For my Amazon woman."

"Indonesia is in the South China Sea, dear." Jessica took the clubs and slung them over her shoulder. "How about you guys, Sam? Have you done any fun family trips lately?"

Sam took a battered bag from Tom. "We went to Mexico this summer, which was fun. It was just for vacation though." Tom grabbed the final bag, closed the back of the vehicle, and the three of them started back. A beep signaled the locking of the doors. "And we took the kids to Disney World a few years ago. Honestly, work is so busy right now that I'm not sure we'll get away for a big vacation this summer unless things really slow down."

A text message notification dinged loudly, and all three adults checked their phones. Jessica held hers up. "It's mine." She tapped the screen and quickly read the text. "Whit's back home with Will. They want to know if they can order pizza for lunch."

Tom peered over her shoulder and read the message. "That's fine. Did she say how it went?"

"They got them all delivered."

"Good."

Sam was trying to imagine Kyle and Hannah partnering on a project and then grabbing lunch afterward. The picture wouldn't form. *Never going to happen.* "What were they doing?"

Jessica's fingers flew over her phone as she texted a reply. "We spent yesterday making some meals for a few families at our church. Two had surgery, one had a baby, and three are shut-ins." She slipped her phone back into her purse. "So the two non-golfers got the job of delivering all of them this morning."

I'm golfing with a family of Mother Teresas.

Tom gestured at Sam's truck as they approached. "Is this you?"

"Yep." Sam handed Wyatt's clubs to Tom and opened the door to the backseat. He grabbed his golf bag and hoisted it onto his shoulder.

"I think I'll grab Wyatt, and the two of us will meet you at the driving range. Does that sound good?" Jessica asked.

Tom nodded. "Works for me." He flashed a wicked smile at his wife. "Since you're getting Wyatt, you get these." He cheerfully dropped their son's clubs onto his wife's other shoulder.

Jessica shoved her purse into his arms. "Then you get this."

"No! Give me the clubs!"

"Ha! Not a chance." Jessica danced out of his reach. "Thanks, babe. Don't use my lipstick!" She set off at a clip.

Sam laughed and raised his eyebrows. "Amazon, huh?"

"Small and fierce anyway." Tom motioned to Sam's clubs. "You golf much?"

Sam locked his truck and the two of them began to make their way to the range. "As much as I can. I try to get out every week when the weather is nice." His consistency had paid off too. His game had improved dramatically over the past several months. "How about you?"

Tom shook his head. "Nah, Jess is the golfer. Something about high-school muscle memory. And Wyatt's decent." He held up his hands in surrender. "Truth be told, I'm actually pretty terrible. They bring me along for entertainment."

Sam chuckled. "Entertainment has its uses."

Tom grinned. "So they tell me."

* * *

The house seemed strangely quiet when Sam walked in the door at seven. He found Nicole alone, curled up on the couch under a blanket with her nose in a book. He wasn't entirely sure she'd want to talk to him, but she looked up when he walked into the living room. Small favors. "Where are the kids?"

Nicole pointed above her head. "Upstairs. Kyle has a History paper due Monday, and Hannah is watching a movie on her tablet." She reached for her bookmark. "Abby's sick. She started running a fever this afternoon, so I put her straight to bed after supper."

Sam frowned. "What does she have?"

Nicole shook her head and closed the novel. "I don't know, a virus? Her fever is 101, so I'm hoping it's too low to be the flu. I gave her some medicine to help keep it down."

Sam leaned on the arm of the couch and looked at his wife. Her eyes were tired, and she looked a little pale. "Are you getting sick too? You look a little run-down."

As soon as the words were out of his mouth, he knew they'd been a mistake.

"Gee, thanks." Nicole snapped open her book and settled deeper into the couch. "I'm fine. How was golf?"

The question was a formality. He knew she hated how much time he spent on the course. "It was good. We got a dinner invitation."

That perked her interest. "From who?"

"Can I sit?" He gestured to her legs filling up most of the couch.

Nicole gave him a begrudging look and tucked them up. "Sure."

Sam sank into the cushions. He rested his hand on her leg and felt her tense. She really was furious at him. Well, maybe this little olive branch would help. "Do you remember a family at the kids' school—the Millers?"

"Jessica's family?"

Leave it to Nicole to know who they were right away. Granted, she'd been much more involved with Heritage when the kids were little than he had. "Yeah, Jessica and Tom. Three kids, two boys and a girl."

Nicole frowned. "I thought they moved. Are they back?"

"They never left. They left Heritage and started homeschooling."

"Really? Huh." Nicole closed her book again. He took that as a good sign she was interested in what he was saying. "Were they there?"

"They were the rest of my group. Tom, Jessica, and their oldest son." He gently pulled her foot into his lap. "Do you remember Wyatt? He played baseball with Tyler."

"I remember, but I'm surprised you do."

Sam didn't rise to the bait. He pressed his thumb onto the ball of her foot and started moving in slow circles. "Well, we spent the afternoon together and had a really good time. They want to have us over for dinner soon." He ran his finger down to her heel. "Jessica said she'd love to reconnect with you and see the kids. I thought we might try and do it when Tyler's home since he and Wyatt might like to catch up too." Sam snuck a glance at Nicole's face. She looked bemused and also, a little pleased. He'd take it.

"That sounds nice." Her voice had lost some of its edge. Sam breathed a small sigh of relief. Nicole leaned over to set her book on the coffee table. "I always liked Jessica, but we never spent much time together. What are they like?"

"Funny. They like to tease each other," Sam said, his mind straying back to the way Tom and Jessica had ribbed each other gently throughout the golf game. "Tom's a terrible golfer." He grinned. "I'm not being mean, that's how he described himself. But we had a great time anyway. Between the rest of us, our score was decent."

Nicole drew her blanket closer around her. "Well, that will be fun. Did you get their phone number? I'll ask her if I can bring something."

Sam laid her foot in his lap and moved to the other one. "I gave them my business card and wrote your number on the back. She said she'd call this week." He slowly rotated her ankle. "Full disclosure, they're a little odd."

Nicole's eyebrows shot up. "Odd how?"

"Not in a bad way. They're just—" Sam struggled to describe them. "Nicely weird, I guess."

"Nicely weird?"

Sam angled his body towards hers. "They are extremely angelic."

"What?" Nicole's half-smiled. "What does that even mean?"

"No, seriously." Sam tried to explain. "They don't go on family vacations. They take *mission trips* instead. And they're all very close. Really close. They spent yesterday making a bunch of meals and then their two youngest kids went off together and delivered them this morning." He let out a low laugh. "And then when we finished the game, they invited me to pray with them."

"Why?"

"I guess they had a really good time?" Sam had been completely befuddled by the invitation.

"What did you do?"

"What could I do? I prayed! I couldn't be the guy who sends his kids to a Christian school, golfs with three actual saints, and then says, 'No thanks, I'll just be going now.'"

Nicole laughed.

Sam's heart warmed. "And it wasn't just the parents. You know who led the prayer? Wyatt."

Nicole swallowed her laughter, her eyes bright. "Okay. Nicely weird sounds about right."

They were both silent for a moment.

Sam cleared his throat. "I know you're upset with me, and I know I've been gone a lot lately." She didn't correct him, but she didn't pull away either. He squeezed her calf and looked at her. "I really am sorry. I know we need to do something different, but I'm honestly not sure what."

Nicole slid her foot out of his lap and tucked her legs back up. "Something's off, Sam." Her voice was sad rather than angry.

Sam's stomach twinged with guilt.

"I know." Sam stood up and stretched. "This family—they're different. I thought maybe spending an evening with them might help us figure out what they're doing."

"Maybe." Nicole rubbed her eyes and sighed.

Sam motioned toward their bedroom with his head. "Want to watch something?"

"We can try. I can't promise to make it very late," Nicole said, pulling the blanket off herself and sliding off the couch.

"I make a good pillow." Sam took the blanket from her and folded it into a tight square, tucking it into a storage ottoman on the other side of the living room. He pulled Nicole into his arms, resting his chin on top of her head. "I love you, you know."

She didn't resist, and he felt her lean into his embrace. Her voice was barely a whisper. "I know. Me too."

CHAPTER 3

Nicole pulled down the passenger side visor and flipped open the small mirror set into the flap. "Do I look okay?" She ran a finger under her left eye and flicked away a dried speck of mascara.

Sam reached behind him and grasped his seatbelt. "You look great."

"You didn't even look."

"You always look great." Sam secured the buckle with a *click* and adjusted the strap across his chest. "Besides, it's just dinner. You're not meeting the queen."

Nicole pushed the visor up and leaned back into her seat. She glanced at her watch. "Hannah needs to hurry. We're supposed to be there in ten minutes."

Sam laid his hand on the SUV's horn and beeped it twice. Five seconds later, the door connecting the garage to the house opened and Hannah stepped out, hopping on one foot as she pulled on her second boot. "I'm coming. You don't have to honk at me!"

Sam rolled down his window. "We gotta go, and you're the only one not in the car. Let's move it!"

Hannah rolled her eyes at him and stood up, boot secure. She stepped back inside for a moment and reemerged with a blue zip-up sweatshirt in hand, slipping her arms through the sleeves as she walked to the vehicle. She gave Sam a look of pure annoyance.

"Drop the attitude with your dad, Hannah. I mean it," Nicole warned as her daughter plopped onto the seat next to Abby. "We told you what time we had to leave. You were the one who chose to start getting ready too late."

"I started getting ready at the same time as Kyle," Hannah grumbled. "And you're not freaking out at him."

"No one is freaking out," Nicole corrected. "And Kyle was ready on time."

"That's because I don't spend twenty minutes on my hair," Kyle said from the seat in the far back.

Hannah whirled around and swung her hand at him.

"*That's enough!*" Sam reached behind him and yanked Hannah back into her seat. "Sit down and knock it off." He pointed at Kyle. "Don't goad her. She'll make you miserable."

Hannah bit her lip, hazel eyes shining with tears. "He started it."

Nicole sighed and rubbed the bridge of her nose. "Everybody stop. Let's just focus on having a nice evening together, please."

Tyler grinned in amusement on the bench next to Kyle. "Ahhhh, family. I've missed you all so much. It's good to be home." He pulled out his phone and opened an app. "Happy Birthday to me!"

"Your birthday was yesterday so we don't have to be nice to you any-more," Kyle said, pulling out his own phone and checking a text. He glanced up to the front of the car and saw his father glare at him. "Just joking, Dad. Jeez."

Sam made a frustrated growl under his breath and muttered something that sounded like, "Not funny."

Nicole slumped deeper into her seat and looked at her husband. "Can we just go? I really don't want to be late." She was already tired, and they hadn't even left the garage yet.

Sam shifted into reverse and slowly backed into the driveway.

Nicole propped her elbow onto the inside of the door beside the window and leaned her cheek into her palm. She should be happy that they were finally all back together again and doing something as a family, but the joy of having the six of them under one roof was still tinged with disappointment. Her eyes darted to the rearview mirror, and she looked at each of her children riding in the back. All four were staring at screens, Abby on her tablet and the rest on their phones.

And that's the way it had been since Tyler had come home. Every time she turned around, someone had been glued to some kind of device. She had hoped that Tyler and Kyle would take the initiative to spend some time together as brothers, but so far there hadn't been much of an opportunity. Kyle had a football game the night of Tyler's birthday and had skipped dinner, then he's spent most of this morning catching up on homework. They'd been playing Nintendo together when she had come home from the girls' dance competition in the afternoon, but that wasn't exactly the quality time she'd had in mind.

Tyler seemed happy to be home. He had surprised her with a call the week before, asking if he could come for his birthday weekend. Nicole suspected Sam had probably threatened their son upon pain of death if he didn't come visit soon, and that this was the reason for Tyler's sudden interest in seeing his family, but she was thankful all the same. She looked at Sam out of the corner of her eye. His jaw was set, frustration plainly etched all over his face. She didn't blame him for getting upset with the kids, but she wished his annoyance wasn't always so obvious.

Nicole scrolled through the pictures on her phone absentmindedly. The photo from Mexico slid onto the screen and she paused. If only this picture reflected reality. Tyler and Kyle, arms around each other looking like best friends. Hannah with a wide smile instead of eyes rolling up into her head. Abby clinging happily to her sister's arm as if they'd played the whole day together. And Sam and herself, cheers-ing with drinks in hand, his arm around her waist and hers behind his back looking more in love than ever.

Well, that part wasn't exactly untrue. The love was certainly there. She didn't doubt that. It was just heavily mixed with disappointment and conflicting priorities.

"Hey, Mom," Tyler said, glancing up from his phone and leaning toward the front seat. "What are the names of Wyatt's family again? I don't want to look like an idiot."

"Tom and Jessica are the parents. Whitney is his sister, and Will is his younger brother." Nicole gestured to Sam as he slowed the car at the stop sign. "I know the GPS says to turn on Elm, but Jessica said to take a right here instead. Cypress is faster." Sam braked and cranked the steering wheel to the right.

"Wyatt, Whitney, and Will?" Kyle repeated, a note of mockery in his voice. "So they're the kind of people who name their kids with only one letter. Classy."

"Shut up. Wyatt's cool." Tyler went back to his phone. "And maybe his sister is hot."

"Tyler!" Nicole spun in her seat. "Watch your mouth. Your baby sister's in the car."

Abby didn't even glance up from her tablet. "It's fine, Mom. I know what hot means already."

Kyle wasn't ready to give up his commentary. "Good thing they stopped at three kids. What 'W' names are left? Wolfgang? Wendy? The baby-name books are slim." He nudged Tyler's knee with his own. "Maybe if they'd had twins, they would have named them Winston and Winifred and had a 'Win-Win' situation."

Tyler and Hannah laughed, and even Sam cracked a smile. Nicole felt the corner of her mouth turn up. "Okay, okay, joke's over. Don't make fun of the family who kindly invited us over and is feeding all six of us." She pointed at Kyle. "Keep the jokes to a minimum. They don't know you well enough to unleash your full humor on them."

"No one's ready for that. I'm a force of nature," Kyle smirked.

The SUV traveled down Cypress Street until the road forked to the left. Sam took the new road—Crestwood—until they reached another stop sign. Nicole read the directions Jessica had given her over the phone. "Take a left here onto Sandalwood, and then a right onto Juniper. Their house is the third on the right."

Sam obeyed the directions she gave and slowed the car in front of a single-story ranch-style house painted in various shades of blue. Nicole was a bit surprised. If she remembered correctly, Tom worked at a hospital or medical office of some kind and had put three kids into private school. The house was newer and seemed nice enough, but it wasn't what she'd expected. Maybe it was bigger on the inside.

The kids piled out of the SUV, and Nicole closed the passenger door behind her. She pulled her cardigan tighter to her body and shivered. It was getting colder at night. Soon an extra layer wouldn't be enough, and they'd be wearing their winter coats whenever they needed to venture outside. Abby slid her hand into Nicole's, and she squeezed it. They all followed Sam up the paved walkway and knocked on the large, white door. A loud bark sounded from inside.

The door opened and a huge golden retriever bounded out to greet them, barking with joy. Abby shrieked and clung to her mother, her nails digging into Nicole's arm.

"Sit! *Sit!*" A blond boy with a splash of freckles across his nose and his arm in a cast grabbed hold of the dog's collar and pulled. The dog whined and thrashed, tail wagging rapidly from one side to the other. "Whit, I can't do this one-handed!"

"Will, Mom said to put him in the back, remember? He gets too excited." A dark-haired girl came running into the entryway and took the dog from her brother, who disappeared back inside the house. She gave them a welcoming smile. "Hi, sorry about that. I'm Whitney." She gestured to the dog. "He's still a puppy, believe it or not. We're trying to train him but it's a slow process."

Nicole disentangled herself from Abby's clutches and stepped off the porch and into the house. "Oh, it's okay. It happens." The dog wagged harder and stood up on his hind legs. "He's very cute."

"Cool dog." Kyle nodded as Whitney pushed him down onto all fours. "What's his name?"

"Winston."

Kyle's mouth twitched.

Tyler coughed to cover a laugh.

Nicole shot them a look that said *Don't-you-dare.*

Whitney grinned. "He was a Christmas present last year. No one expected him to get so big." She kept her fingers looped under Winston's collar as she walked backward into the house. "Come on, boy. Outside."

"Well, he seems like a *wonderfully winsome* animal," Kyle said solemnly as Whitney led the way into an open concept living space, dragging Winston behind her.

Sam clapped his hand on Kyle's shoulder, and Nicole watched him tighten his grip in a squeeze.

"Worth it," Kyle said, offering his father's stony face a big smile. Sam gave him a small shove, and the family traipsed into the living room.

"Welcome!" Jessica waved them over from where she was standing behind the kitchen sink, a knife in one hand. "I'm finishing the salad." She set the blade on the counter and wiped her hands on a dishtowel. "It's so good to see you guys. Will, can you take their coats please?"

Nicole smiled. "Thank you so much for inviting us."

"Our pleasure. It's been too long." Jessica gave her a quick hug. "Whitney, can you call the guys up?" She turned to Nicole. "They're in the basement."

Whitney put Winston outside and closed the door. Through the large bay window overlooking a wooden deck and the backyard beyond, they could see Winston plainly moping.

Jessica clasped her hands in front of her. "I know Nicole and Sam," she said, pointing at Tyler, who was shrugging out of his sweatshirt so he could hand it to Will's waiting arm. "And I'm guessing you're the one who played with Wyatt."

"Tyler. Nice to meet you."

Nicole was happy to see Tyler offered his hand, and Jessica shook it.

"Which makes you Kyle." Jessica shook his hand next.

"Guilty," Kyle said. "I like your entryway."

"That was Tom's project. It's one of his favorite parts of the house." Jessica moved on to Hannah, who quietly said hello and thanked her for the dinner invitation. She stopped in front of Abby, who still had her hand tightly clamped to Nicole's.

"And that means that you must be Abby." Jessica crouched down to see Abby eye-to-eye. "You were pretty tiny the last time I saw your family, so I'm not sure we've ever officially met. I'm Miss Jessica."

Abby smiled shyly and gave a little wave. "Hi."

"Hi there." Jessica grinned and stood up. She glanced at Nicole. "I bet everyone tells you how much she looks like you."

"They do, but she gets the red hair from Sam," Nicole said, feeling herself relax. Jessica was the sort of person who put her at ease. Bouncy, personal, genuine. She was last to hand Will her cardigan, piling it on top of his one good arm. He exited the living room and down a hallway.

Tom appeared at the top of the staircase leading down to the basement, followed closely by Wyatt. "Hey, you made it!" Tom said. "Sorry, we got distracted by a cutthroat ping-pong tournament." He motioned to Wyatt. "Unlike our golf game, I won."

Introductions began again, and Nicole found herself looking back at the entryway to see what had caused Kyle's comment. A large cross spread across the wall, the shelf beneath it filled with various books. Family photographs hung to the sides of the cross, but Nicole couldn't make out what was in the frames. The display was prominent, and she realized that it was the first thing that any guest would see when they entered the house. That is, unless Winston bowled them over first.

"You guys are probably starving," Jessica said, taking the salad bowl from the countertop and fishing a pair of tongs out of a drawer. "Dinner's ready, so we can eat whenever. I made spaghetti."

Abby beamed at her. "That's my favorite! Do you have bread?"

"Bread and dessert." Wyatt pointed to a trifle dish piled high with what looked like Oreo cookies drowning in pudding and whipped cream. "Whitney and Will made it."

"Um, I think you mean *I* made it," Will said, entering the living room with his hands free. "Whitney was supposed to help, but her babysitting job ran late." He gave the dish a look of appraisal and shrugged. "I promise it tastes better than it looks. I'm not usually left-handed."

"It looks great." Hannah was looking at Will with an anxious look on her face. "I bet it's really good."

"Shall we?" Tom slid an arm around his wife's shoulders. "I call dibs on the biggest heel."

***

"That was amazing," Nicole said as she picked up her plate and followed Jessica behind the counter to the sink. "I'd love that sauce recipe if you're willing to share it."

"It's Tom's dad's recipe. He made it up, and it's become the family staple." Jessica scraped a smattering of noodles off her plate and into the garbage disposal. "I'll email it to you."

Nicole walked back to the table and gathered up the remaining plates and silverware. Tom and Sam were already in the living room, sodas in hand, swapping work stories. Nicole hadn't seen Sam so relaxed in ages. She watched him talk, hands outstretched to show the dimensions of something in his story. Tom threw back his head and laughed, and Nicole felt her stomach drop in a strange mix of joy and jealousy. She took an empty water glass from the table and set it on top of the stack of plates.

Tyler and Wyatt had hit it off immediately and disappeared onto the back deck, then down the stairs to the backyard. Nicole could see a fire pit in one corner of the lot, its flames dancing a flickering light over the two of them playing a game of cornhole. The rest of the kids had ventured downstairs to play two-on-two ping-pong and, in Abby's case, explore an old doll house of Whitney's. Their laughs floated upstairs every few minutes, and Nicole breathed a sigh of contentment. They were all happy. Even if it were just for an evening.

"So, Hannah said she's into dance." Jessica glanced up from the salad bowl she was scrubbing. "What kind?"

"She's done a few different things, but ballet is her favorite." Nicole picked up the plates, carefully balancing six forks and two cups on the top of them. "She loves it, but to be honest, it's wearing on me." She looked at the pile of dishes waiting to be washed. "Can I help?"

"Want to dry?" Jessica gestured to a red towel lying on the countertop. "That one should work." She offered Nicole an encouraging smile. "So, what's wearing you out?"

Nicole set the plates next to the sink. "Oh, just the schedule. When Hannah was little, she had practice once a week, and it was something her little friends were all doing. Plus, it got me out of the house when Abby was a baby." She picked up the drying towel. "She was a natural, so she started competing when she was in second grade, and it's just gotten busier from there. Now she's in practice three days a week after school and competing once or twice a month." Nicole took the bowl from Jessica and began wiping it dry. "She's good though. The dance studio puts on *The Nutcracker* every other year, and last December she danced the role of Clara even though she was only eleven. I know it's not the New York City Ballet or anything, but it was still a really big honor."

Jessica opened the dishwasher and began loading the rinsed silverware. "That's a huge honor. She must have loved it."

Nicole nodded. "She did. It made for a crazy Christmas though." She paused, her hand stilling over the salad bowl. "Can I ask you something?"

"Of course," Jessica said.

Nicole twisted the towel in her hand, suddenly shy. "I'm not actually sure how to say this."

"Oh great, did Tom offend you by offering you wine? I told him not to do that until we knew you better."

"What? Oh, no. Nothing like that." Nicole shook her head. "I just don't know how to put it into words."

Jessica straightened and turned the sink back on, water cascading into the basin as she started on the stack of dishes. "I'm pretty much an open book and I'm hard to offend, so go for it," Jessica said.

Nicole was silent for a moment, a furrow forming between her brows as she gathered her thoughts. She set the dry salad bowl onto a dish mat and picked up a stockpot. "How did you all get so close?"

Jessica cocked her head. "You mean as a family?"

"Yes," Nicole said, rubbing the inside of the pot. She'd watched them carefully over dinner and had been surprised to see that Sam was right. The bonds in the family were strong, and it wasn't just the parents. That Tom and Jessica had a solid marriage was obvious, but the three Miller kids all seemed to genuinely enjoy each other's company as well. They were either excellent actors or were truly close, and Nicole suspected it was the latter. "Honestly, most of my friends with kids around this age are going from one thing to another and are hardly ever home all at once." She motioned to the dining table. "Is this a normal thing for you, having everyone home for supper? I can't even imagine how many things we would have to stop doing to make that happen."

Jessica crossed to the stovetop and flicked on a gas burner. Flames leapt to life beneath a blue tea kettle. "Well, homeschooling definitely helps with keeping a less hectic schedule, but I realize that's not for everyone." She went back to the sink and began sliding plates into the dishwasher. "Whit and Will are both early risers, so they're usually done with their schoolwork by lunch, and we've set some limits on how much time they can spend on their hobbies and extra activities because we want them to be home most evenings." She wrestled an oddly shaped pasta turner onto the top rack. "As for dinner, yes and no. We eat together most nights, but usually it's just the four of us now that Wyatt's not living at home."

Clang. Nicole dropped the ladle she'd been drying. "Wyatt doesn't live here?"

"No, he moved out back in February. We all thought it would be a good idea for him to get some real-world experience living on his own."

Jessica popped a soap pod into the dishwasher and closed the door, tapping two buttons to start the machine. "He has three roommates, and they're all sharing a two-bedroom apartment." She chuckled. "It's a bit crowded when they're all there sleeping or studying, but it's still bigger than a dorm."

Nicole looked out the back window again. Wyatt and Tyler were still playing cornhole, bean bags flying in clean arcs over the grass. "Did he just come home to see us?"

Jessica rinsed soapy water out of the Dutch oven that had held the spaghetti sauce. "Not exactly. I mean, he was certainly looking forward to seeing Tyler." She handed the pot to Nicole. It was the last dish to dry. "He actually comes over every Friday night for supper."

"Really?" Nicole was astonished. "Isn't Friday night when all his friends go out?" A sudden thought occurred to her. "Or...is it something you guys have asked him to do so that he doesn't go out and party?" Tyler's face flashed through her mind.

Jessica shook her head. "Nothing like that. When Wyatt moved out, we told him he was welcome to come over any time and that we were still going to have Family Fridays." She leaned against the counter and wiped her hands on a dry towel. "For years, Friday was always our family night. Sometimes we'd have friends over, other times we'd have a picnic dinner in front of a movie, you get the idea. Anyway—" Jessica crossed her arms. "We told Wyatt that we were still going to do Family Fridays and that he was always welcome. And so far, he's pretty much chosen to come home for them."

Nicole tried to wrap her mind around the reality of having a college-aged son who was more interested in coming home for a family dinner than going out with his friends. But then, she realized that even if Tyler had wanted to drive an hour home every Friday night, the rest of them would likely be scattered to the four winds and he'd arrive at an empty house. It wasn't exactly an open invitation.

Jessica watched her closely, and Nicole tried to smile. "That really is wonderful," Nicole said. "It's obvious you guys gave him something sweet to come home to." The wistfulness in her voice was raw, and she hated it. "I wish Tyler felt that way. But I guess I can't blame him if he doesn't."

"What do you mean?"

"Well, we're hardly ever home for dinner all at once," Nicole said, heat rising in her cheeks. It was never something that embarrassed her before, so why was she feeling so ashamed right now? She struggled to explain. "I mean, between Kyle's practices and games and the girls' dance practices..." Her voice trailed off. "And Sam works a lot of overtime." She heard the words tumbling out of her mouth and stopped, the reality of her life hitting her squarely between the eyes. "I guess I answered my own question. We're just too busy to be together."

Jessica looked at her with compassion in her gaze. "Is that something you and Sam want to change? Or is it just a hard stage of life for you right now?"

The teakettle whistled, and Nicole jumped.

Jessica turned off the burner and moved the kettle to a cooler part of the stove. "Do you want some tea?" She opened the cabinet to the right of the stove and motioned to its contents. "I also have hot chocolate and the kind of apple cider that's really just a packet of sugar."

Anything to warm up the icy guilt flaring in her stomach. "I'd love some tea. Do you have peppermint?"

Jessica grabbed two teabags from a box and dropped them into mugs, the smell of peppermint wafting into the air as the steaming water poured over them. She handed one cup to Nicole and took the other for herself. "Want to sit?"

Nicole nodded and Jessica led the way back to the dining table.

Nicole slid onto a chair and plunked her mug onto the wooden surface of the table. She stroked the side of the cup with her fingertips. "I feel really ridiculous talking to you about this." She glanced up at Jessica. "I mean, we haven't seen each other for years, and here I'm telling you all kinds of personal stuff."

Jessica took a sip of her tea, a look of thoughtfulness in her blue eyes. "I think sometimes it's easier to talk to someone you don't know very well about stuff like this. But we can stop if you want."

"No, it's good. I'd love some perspective or advice, if you're willing." Nicole took a deep breath and sighed. "Sam doesn't seem to think anything is wrong. He knows we're in a bit of a rut, but he isn't worried about it. I think he assumes everything will just work itself out." Her thoughts strayed to Tyler, and she closed her eyes. "But I know something isn't right. And I'm afraid that if we don't figure out what it is and fix it, we're going to have some serious regrets."

Jessica propped her elbow onto the table and rested her chin in her palm. "Have you talked to your pastor about it?"

"Ahhhh...." Well, another elephant in the room. Nicole frantically counted backward. How many weeks had it been since they'd been in church?

Jessica seemed to realize that she'd touched on an uncomfortable subject. She fiddled with the tag of her teabag. "Do you guys still go to Breakthrough? I heard they got a new pastor."

They had, but their attendance had been so sporadic that Nicole was blanking on his name. Something with a J. James maybe? Or Josh?

"His name is Phil, right?"

Phil. Not a J.

"Yeah, I think so." Nicole took another sip of tea. "Honestly, we haven't been as regular as we should be." It was so much of an understatement that it was almost a lie. She could probably count on one hand the number of times they'd made it to church since school let out for the summer, and Thanksgiving was three weeks away.

Jessica drummed her fingers on the side of her mug. "Well, I don't know if you're open to going to a different church, but ours offers a really good parenting class that might help you work through how you're feeling." She waved a hand through the air. "I say this with zero pressure, I just thought you might be interested. You can do it one-on-one or with a small group."

"Have you taken it?"

"Tom and I took it years ago and really enjoyed it. It helped us be more intentional with each other and with our kids." Jessica sat back in her chair. "We had some similar struggles to what you're describing and wanted to change some things."

"And it helped?" Nicole felt hope stir.

"It did, but it's not really something that one parent can do without the other." Jessica's eyes flickered to Sam. "In order to really make it worthwhile, Sam would need to be on board."

The small flame of hope sputtered and died.

Nicole gave a humorless laugh. Sam regularly going to church and taking a class with her to improve their parenting? He'd sooner become a vegetarian.

"Pray about it," Jessica said, understanding written plainly across her features. "You never know. He might surprise you."

***

"Dude, it *sucks*." Tyler lobbed a blue bean bag through the air. It sailed cleanly onto the corn-hole board and slid to a stop, just short of the opening. "Dang. Okay, knock me in."

"Don't count on it." Wyatt threw his own bag, and it plopped directly into the hole with ease, barely touching the sides of the wooden board. "What's so bad about it? From what your parents said at dinner, you have a lot of friends."

"Nah." Tyler shook his head, squeezing the next bag in his hand as he took aim. "Not really friends, just teammates."

"Is there a difference?"

"Oh, yeah." Tyler tossed the bag and it hit the corner of the board, then flopped off into the grass. He didn't want to elaborate. "College just isn't at all what I expected."

Wyatt sailed a red bag through the air, landing another clean shot into the hole. "How about your classes?"

Tyler shrugged. School had always come easy to him, and so far, college was the same. But easy and interesting weren't the same thing—and often, even at odds with each other. "They're okay, I guess. I'm really just taking all the Gen Ed requirements right now, so it's not like I'm learning about anything I actually want to do."

Wyatt moved a bag from hand to hand. "Which is what?"

Tyler shrugged again. "No idea. But Gen Ed isn't giving me any revelations, I can tell you that much." He threw too hard this time, and his bag whizzed over to the wooden fence surrounding the backyard. "Ugh, I should never have quit baseball." He glanced at Wyatt. "What about you? Are you just doing Gen Ed too?"

Wyatt shook his head. "I'm at Devon Falls Tech, so my classes are focused on what I want to do for a living already. Plus, I'm doing an

internship with an HVAC company, so a lot of my learning is on-the-job."
His third bag landed with a *thunk* in the middle of the board.

"You want to fix air conditioners?" Tyler worked to keep the skepticism out of his voice. Wyatt was way too cool for something almost-lame.

Wyatt laughed. "It's not so much about the air conditioners as it is the kind of work I like. And they cooperate with my program so my schedule is flexible around my classes." He pointed at the cornhole board. "This time, arc it higher but use a little less force. You're close."

Tyler adjusted his grip and did his best to incorporate Wyatt's advice. The bag slipped from his fingers, flipped through the air, and landed half-in-half-out of the hole.

Wyatt grinned.

Tyler stood back and waited for Wyatt to finish his turn. "It's a little sickening how good you are at this." Wyatt's bag flipped through the air and knocked Tyler's into the hole completely, tumbling in after it. "Thanks for that. You still crushed me, ten to four."

The two of them walked across the grass to collect the bean bags. "HVAC techs get to work with their hands, which I like," Wyatt said. "And I can pretty much go anywhere with my skills. A lot of people don't like to work out in bad weather, but I've never minded it so that's not a turn off for me. Plus, there's lots of overtime."

"Aren't you afraid of not having a business degree or at least a bachelor's or something?" Tyler wondered. "I've always heard that having one sort of guarantees a higher paying job so you can pay off your student loans faster."

"Nah, not at all. I mean, my cousin got a teaching degree and then decided to become a mechanic. And my uncle got a master's in criminal science and ended up running a big chain of hardware stores and made a ton of money." Wyatt picked up the lone blue bag over by the fence and threw it to Tyler. "I actually looked it up a while ago. Only about a fourth of college grads end up using their major in their job, so I don't feel like I'm missing anything." He spread his hands. "And I don't have any student loans."

"Seriously?" Tyler didn't even want to think about how much he had had to borrow, and that was after he won an academic scholarship. He winced. Which he might not even have next year if he kept making stupid choices.

"If you don't really like what you're doing, why don't you talk to your parents? They might be cool with you taking a gap year or something."

"I can't talk to them." Tyler deposited the bean bags in a storage sack. "My dad will say I'm wasting my potential and that I need to grow up. And my mom will get all weepy and wonder where she went wrong that she's raised a college dropout as a son. Then they'll end up in a fight, as usual." He shoved his hands into the pockets of his sweatshirt. "And what would I even say? It's not like I know what I want to do if I quit."

Wyatt zipped up the bag. "I guess it could be worth sticking out for a little longer anyway. You never know, you might take a class that really connects with you and gives you some direction."

"Maybe." Why did that prospect make him depressed?

The back door opened, and Hannah's head popped out, ponytail swinging. "Tyler, Dad says we have to go."

"I'll be there in a sec!" Tyler gestured to the cornhole boards. "Seriously, thanks man. It was good to see you. Even if you did completely annihilate my game."

Wyatt laughed and clapped him on the shoulder. "Guess that just means you'll have to come back to teach me a lesson."

***

"I didn't say weird. I said nicely weird."

Nicole stood at the bathroom sink, toothbrush in hand, a frown forming between her brows. "What's the difference?"

Sam was already in bed holding the television remote. He clicked a button and Netflix popped onto the screen. He scrolled through program options. "Nicely weird is fine. Plain weird is bad."

Nicole rinsed her toothbrush and set the electric handle back on its stand. She took the cup next to the sink and swished her mouth, trying to choose her next words carefully. "I guess I don't understand why you don't think they're just 'nice' without the 'weird' qualification."

Sam sat up and adjusted his pillow. "To be fair, I said that after the golf tournament, not after dinner tonight. I had a good time. They're nice." He paused. "They're nice with some weird ideas, is that fine?"

Nicole flipped the light switch, dousing the bathroom in darkness as she crossed the room and grabbed a hairbrush from the top of her dresser. "I didn't really hear any weird ideas from Jessica. They're different from us but not strange. Did Tom say something?"

Sam clicked the menu button on the remote and picked another streaming service to peruse. "It wasn't anything bad, Nic. He's a nice guy. We just do life differently."

Nicole ran the brush underneath her hair and pulled, silky strands weaving in between the bristles. "Can you give me an example?"

Sam looked at her out of the corner of his eye before focusing his attention back on the television screen. "Okay, well he told me that he barely works forty hours a week. Apparently, they used to live in a bigger house, and he worked a lot more when the kids were younger." He glanced at Nicole who worked to keep her face impassive. "His dad died a few years ago, and he decided he wanted to spend more time with his family after that, so they decided to downsize and cut back on work. That's around the time they pulled the kids from Heritage Christian." An ad for a newly released film flashed across the screen. "How about this one?"

She didn't care about a movie tonight. "That's fine. So, you think he's weird because he wants to spend more time with his family?" She could hear the vulnerability in her voice and wondered if he did as well.

"No, I think it's weird to purposefully not be ambitious."

Nicole set the brush back on the dresser and slid under the covers, considering his words. "Who says he isn't ambitious?"

Sam waved a hand dismissively in the air. "It's just the feeling I get from him. He's focused on his wife and kids and having a flexible schedule and sure, that's admirable. But that's not how I think."

He shook his head, and Nicole could tell that he was trying not to be defensive.

"I love my family," Sam said. "And I'm supposed to provide for them as well as I can. The more I work, the more I make, and the more options we have for our future. Plus, I don't have the kind of job that offers the flexibility he has."

"What does he do?"

Sam sank back into his pillow and rubbed a hand down his face. "Uhhh...what did he call it? He's a nurse, but he gets to pick his own hours and higher pay because he floats to a bunch of clinics in town."

"Like a PRN?"

"That's it." He clicked *play* on the remote and the screen went black. "We live in different worlds. Even if I wanted to, I couldn't have a schedule like that with my job."

"That's true." But he also didn't have to pull sixty-hour weeks multiple times a month either.

Sam turned up the volume and dropped the remote onto the comforter. "They're nice, honey. But I don't want to be them."

Sadness curled itself around Nicole's heart and settled there. She bit her lip. "I really respect them as parents. I know we were only there for an evening, but they seem so at ease, and they all enjoy each other."

Sam reached behind her head and rested his arm across her shoulders. "Yeah, they do appear to be great parents. Maybe they just got really good kids."

His voice was teasing, and she let out a small laugh. "I asked Jessica how they do it and she mentioned a parenting class at their church that was helpful. Any chance you'd be willing to try something like that?"

The movie title flashed across the screen, and Sam raised his eyebrows. "Honestly, I'm not really interested in a parenting class. I think we're fine."

She wasn't surprised, but the disappointment was there all the same. "Okay, no parenting class. What about trying a different church?" They were delinquent attendees. A change might be the shot in the arm that they needed. "They go to Grace Fellowship, and I've heard good things."

Sam cocked his head noncommittally. "It's not like we're exactly regulars at Breakthrough. I don't mind if you want to try somewhere else." He glanced at her. "Are you wanting to go tomorrow?"

"If we can."

Sam shook his head. "I'm on call all day, and you know how it is this time of year with the weather changing." His face softened. "Take the kids though. If you like it, I'll try to get there next time we want to go."

It wasn't what she'd hoped for, but it was a start. Nicole spread an extra blanket over herself and snuggled in. "What's this movie about?"

Sam grinned at her and winked. "It would be pointless to explain. We both know you'll be asleep in twenty minutes."

CHAPTER 4

Nicole sank into the living room couch cushions with a sigh and tipped her head back onto the overstuffed headrest. Her back twinged, and she winced. It had been a long day, but the dishes were done, the floor was swept, and all the laundry was put away. She glanced at her watch. It was late, and Sam still wasn't home, but to his credit, he had remembered to text today.

Nicole rubbed her forehead. She was thankful he'd let her know of the change in his schedule, but it was the third night this week that he hadn't been home before the kids were all in their rooms for the night. If he didn't hurry, he wouldn't even see Abby today, who was curled up in bed with *On the Banks of Plum Creek* for the final thirty minutes before her bedtime. Kyle and Hannah both had homework and would be up for a little bit, but a quick hello in the middle of a History paper or Math lesson was hardly what she considered quality time with their father.

Her eyes landed on the pamphlet on the edge of the end table, and she reached for it. *The Family Journey* was printed in cheerful script across the top of the brochure. Below the title, a photo of a family hiking through a forest covered the rest of the front flap, the focal point showing a father smiling at his son as they passed a water bottle between them. Nicole flicked open to the first page and skimmed the summary of the class. She'd read the brochure on Sunday afternoon after Jessica had pressed it into her hands after church, and again on Wednesday as she'd waited in the carpool line after school before shuttling the girls to dance. It was as though by rereading she might find the secret for how to entice disinterested husbands into taking the class. So far, no such luck.

Nicole fiddled with the corner of the pamphlet. Going to church had been interesting. Sam had been right: He had been called into work an hour before they left, but she had managed to bring the younger three kids with her without too much complaining. Tyler had opted to sleep in after staying up late gaming with a friend from high school, and Nicole hadn't felt comfortable insisting that he come along when he was an adult living on his own. Most of all, she didn't want to annoy him into staying away from home, and so she hadn't pushed.

Grace Fellowship was different than Breakthrough. The music was simple rather than concert-like, and they had even sung some hymns. It was a smaller congregation, but friendly and active. Nicole had a feeling that if they'd been attending regularly and stopped, someone would have noticed and called. But the biggest surprise had been the sermon itself, which had been a thorough explanation of Psalm 134. Nicole had no idea that so much goodness could be extracted from so few verses. At Breakthrough, they focused on stories. Often the pastor wouldn't even open his Bible, choosing to paraphrase the content instead and explain how it applied to the lives of the congregation. But this pastor had the Scriptures open the entire time, continually going back to them and pulling in other verses to show how things connected. Nicole had never heard anything like it.

She heard the garage door activate and a minute later, Sam walked into the house with a bag from Chick-Fil-A crumpled in his left hand. He looked haggard and exhausted, but he flashed a smile her way when he saw she was looking at him. "Hey, babe. Whatcha reading?"

"Just that pamphlet." She had left it in plain view all week. She'd seen him flip through it for all of thirty seconds before dropping it back onto the table.

"Oh, that again? You know, they make longer ones now. I think they're called books." Nicole heard the tease in his voice as Sam walked over to the garbage can and stuffed the empty fast-food bag inside. He stopped beneath the archway connecting the living room to the kitchen and leaned against the wall. "Good day?"

"Long day. Even the kids seemed tired at dinner." She fought the temptation to mention his absence. Instead, she closed the pamphlet and creased the sides. "I'm not really up for a movie tonight, but is there any chance we could talk for a little bit?"

Sam glanced behind him at the fridge and shrugged. "If I can do it with a beer, sure. But can we go downstairs?" He nodded toward the basement. "If you want to go to sleep, I'll just watch TV down there so you can hit the hay."

Nicole felt a stab of annoyance, immediately followed by a sense of shame. He was trying to be considerate, and she knew it. But his disinterest was obvious, and it stung. She took a deep breath and stood from the couch as a beer bottle hissed. Sam wasted no time.

The door to the basement was already open, and Nicole followed her husband down the wooden, hopefully-soon-to-be-carpeted stairs. Sam flicked on the light at the bottom of the stairwell and light flooded into the oversized open space. When they'd bought the house, only the right side of the basement had been finished. A small hallway led to an extra bedroom, a bathroom, and a tiny office that Nicole claimed as her craft room before opening into a nice-sized living space that Sam had declared his Man Cave. The left side of the basement was framed, but unfinished, and in his small amounts of spare time, Sam had been working on making the large open area their family room. He'd done most of the electrical work already, but there was still sheetrock and texturing to do before painting and carpeting. He didn't allow the kids downstairs much with all the wiring exposed, but their old couch had found a home in the center of the room and pointed directly at a large TV.

Nicole curled up in one corner of the couch and wished she'd thought to bring down a blanket. Sam sat beside her, pushing aside a box on the floor with his foot. Something clanked inside the cardboard, and Nicole realized that the box was full of the trophies that Tyler had left behind when he went to college. She squinted at the frames leaning up against the television stand. More Tyler awards. Not a thing that was Kyle's or Hannah's or Abby's.

Sadness and anger vied for dominance in her mind, but Nicole rubbed her hands up and down her jeans and worked to keep her voice level. "I wanted to talk about how you think our family is doing?" She tucked a strand of dark hair behind her ear. "When you look at how we act around each other and what we're spending time doing, are you satisfied?"

Sam took a long drink from his bottle and settled back into the couch. "I think we're fine. I don't really have anything to complain about." He looked at her, as if for help. "I mean, Kyle didn't do very well in football this year, but that was because he was injured. Basketball is more his thing anyway, so I'm hoping that goes better." He rested the bottle on his knee. "Obviously I've got some concerns about Tyler, but I think being home was good for him. Maybe it will be enough to help him not make stupid decisions." He was quiet for a moment and then looked at her with a slightly baffled expression. "The girls are doing well in dance, right? I just assume you'll tell me if they're not."

"Dance is going fine. We're just really busy." Sam had never been interested in the girls' activities. Going to dance competitions was his idea of torture.

"Good." Sam shrugged. "Work, the kids, us. Honestly, babe, I know you think we need some sort of intervention, but I look around and think we're fine. Not perfect, but we have a lot of good here. Everyone is healthy, everyone has decent grades, and I'm making plenty of money for the life we have." He raised an eyebrow in her direction. "But I assume that you see things differently since you're asking this question."

Nicole picked at a loose thread in her sleeve. "I'm grateful for all the things you just mentioned. I really am. I just also know we're missing something important too." She struggled to put her thoughts into words. "We're so busy, it's sometimes chaotic. We're more like ships passing each other than a family deepening our relationships. I always thought that as the kids got older, we'd all get closer. But it's the opposite."

"The kids are growing up and becoming more independent, that's all. And with independence comes a busier life."

"I don't think that's it," Nicole said, shaking her head. "I think we have a lot of things going on, and we look healthier to the outside world than we actually are."

Sam stared at her. "What in the world does that mean?"

She knew she wasn't explaining things well. She was too afraid of making him feel attacked. Nicole leaned toward Sam and said gently, "Okay, for example. We send our kids to a Christian school. I think everyone assumes that we must be these strong Christians who really value a Bible-filled education and that we're raising our kids to be firm in their faith. But then I look at what we're actually doing, and I don't see us doing that." Sam opened his mouth to argue, but Nicole pushed forward. "I know we value those *ideas*, but what are we actually doing to make them a reality? We put them in a good school, but are we talking about any of that stuff at home? Are we regularly taking them to church? And before you say I'm overreacting—" Nicole could see the annoyance written plainly across her husband's face. "I want you to think about Tyler. Literally the minute he stepped outside of this house, he's made bad choices and has zero interest in anything to do with faith." She knew her words would hurt, but it was vital that he see the truth of them. "We're missing something."

"We're missing something because our teenage son has been away at college for two months and hasn't been a perfect angel? That's your case?" Sam drained the rest of his bottle and set it firmly on the floor with a *clank*.

"No, that's just part of it. It's also how disconnected we all are."

"Correction: It's how disconnected *you think* we are." He was irritated and it showed. "Have you ever considered that maybe you just are struggling with the kids growing up and not needing you as much because they have their own lives?"

Ouch. Nicole was tempted to snap at him in defense. "I don't think that's it."

Sam rolled his eyes. "Of course not. It has to be a crisis."

Now *that* was uncalled for. "I'm not being dramatic!"

Sam raised his eyebrows. "Who else in this family thinks there's anything wrong? Are the kids unhappy? Am I? You seem to be the only person who thinks there is something off and rather than say, 'Hey, maybe everything is actually fine,' you want to drag the rest of us into therapy."

"That's completely unfair!" The calm she'd fought so hard to maintain was rapidly wearing thin. "I'm not trying to find a problem where one doesn't exist. It's just that ever since we went to the Millers—"

"Oh my word, not them again." Sam ran a hand down his face and let out an exasperated grunt. "If I'd known that going to their house for dinner meant that we'd be compared to them for the rest of our lives, I would have never accepted that invitation."

"I'm not comparing us to them because I want to be them," Nicole said. "I see something in them I think we are missing, and I want to have that too. And you said as much when you came home from that golf tournament!"

"Yeah, but apparently to get it I would have to have a job that lets me work barely full time and downsize my house and tick off my children by pulling them from activities that are important to them. Hard pass." Sam folded his arms across his chest. "And you'd have to homeschool, so have fun with that."

Nicole covered her face with her hands and squeezed her eyes shut in frustration. She took a deep breath and blew it out. "I don't think we have to become exactly like them to have the relationships with our kids that they do. But I don't think what we're doing is working either."

Sam lifted the couch's armrest and scooped out the remote control hidden in the storage compartment. He pressed the power button, and the television turned blue.

She'd lost him.

Sam pressed another button, and a sports channel sprang to life on the screen, displaying a commercial for toothpaste. He turned up the volume. "We've been over this. I have the job I have, and I work the way I do because we need the money. It's just a busier season of life for us right now." He glanced at her face and softened at her defeated expression. "I don't think the solution is to freak out that something must be wrong because it's hard. Instead, we should just push through it and keep going. Eventually things will settle down. We're fine, just relax."

There was nothing more to be said, and the commercial break was ending. Nicole took that as her cue to leave. She stood up from the couch and picked up the beer bottle. Sam would forget to bring it upstairs, and the recycling was getting picked up tomorrow.

She could feel hot tears building inside of her eyes, but she refused to let them fall. He couldn't see the glaring problem she could, no matter how clearly she tried to explain it. They were at an impasse.

Sam muttered something from the couch.

Nicole turned at the bottom of the stairs, unsure she'd heard correctly. "What?"

"Nothing. I was talking to myself."

"Okay. Goodnight." She started climbing, hand sliding gently up the railing. Frustration and helplessness sat heavy in her soul, and a tear spilled onto her cheek. She closed the door at the top of the stairs and leaned her head against it, heart aching. She wiped away the tear and repeated the words to herself that Sam hadn't meant for her to hear. *I'm doing the best I can.*

So was she.

But she couldn't fix this alone.

If Kyle had been a gambling man, he would have bet that this had never happened to Tyler.

He glanced at the clock on the kitchen stove and then at his watch. Both read 10:20, which meant that his dad was a solid twenty minutes later than he'd promised, and if he didn't arrive in the next two, Kyle was going to be officially late for his first basketball game of the season. Wonderful. His coach would be delighted.

He opened his messages app and tapped his dad's contact. A line of blue speech bubbles appeared, one right after another. Kyle drummed his other hand on the counter in annoyance as he read through his texts. The first had been at 10:05. *You on your way?*

There hadn't been a reply.

10:09's text read, *Gotta leave by 10:20 at the latest.*

Still nothing.

At 10:12, he'd called and been unsurprised that the phone had punted him straight to voicemail. Typical.

And the final text at 10:18: *Riding my bike if I don't hear by 10:20.*

Technically, he could call his mom and tell her he needed a ride. She'd probably leave the dance competition and come get him, making him only a few minutes late. There were plenty of other moms who could keep an eye on Hannah and Abby for fifteen minutes or so, and most of the time they were just watching other dancers anyway. But Kyle had decided against that plan when he'd realized that calling his mom meant telling her that his dad had forgotten him. That pretty much guaranteed a giant fight between his parents, and his dad sleeping in the basement again.

So it looked like it was just him and his reliable Schwinn.

Kyle grabbed his jacket and zipped up the front, yanking his backpack off the neighboring barstool and slipping his arms into the straps. Unfortunately, he now had to bike to school on the first day there was frost all over the ground. *Awesome.*

He checked his phone one more time—nothing—and quickly shoved it into a spare zipper pocket on the back of his bag. He ran through a mental checklist as he stepped out into the garage and tugged fingerless gloves onto his hands.

Lights off. *Check.*

Front door locked. *Check.*

Stove off. *Check.*

Basketball gear packed and loaded into the car. *Check-ish.*

Kyle pressed the garage door opener and wheeled his bike out into the sunlight. His breath was frosty in the morning air, and he shivered. His coat was thick, but the chill sliced through it, a bitter breeze ruffling his hair.

Now that he had been denied a heated car ride, a beanie was a must.

Kyle leaned his bike against the house and ran back inside. His mom kept the box of winter hats in the hall closet during the summer and early autumn, and he was pretty sure they'd been so busy that she hadn't thought to bring them out yet. He pulled open the closet door and stuck his head past the coats. There it was. And his favorite grey one was right on top.

He tugged the knitted cap over his head until it properly covered his ears and jogged back through the garage. It was still cold, but the hat helped considerably. Kyle unbuckled his helmet and tried to jam it onto his head. He grunted in frustration, alternating yanking the straps to try and wiggle it over his beanie. His head would not cooperate.

It had to be close to 10:25 now, and it was a ten-minute bike ride to the school. Kyle chucked the helmet into the garage and punched the code into the keypad to close the door. Ten minutes was a short ride that he'd ridden dozens of times. And he was cold. *Hat > Helmet.* If his mom fussed, maybe he'd tell her about his dad after all. It was every man for himself.

Kyle jumped onto the bicycle seat and sped down his driveway, pumping his legs to gain speed as he sailed down Willowbrook Drive. After several blocks, the road forked, and he veered left. Straight would take him toward downtown, but his chosen route would take him around the city park and spit him out four blocks from the high school. He pedaled harder, frustrated at the idea of being late and how he knew the coach would bark at him. As if he could control his parents.

Sharp right onto Allgood.

Left onto Academy.

Another left onto Morningside and up a big hill. *Four blocks to go.*

Traffic was light and Kyle was sweating by the time he reached the top at the corner of Morningside and Crestview. From his vantage point, he could see the roof of the high school gym. A flashing sign across the street displayed the time: 10:31. Well, he'd been fast. Two minutes, and he'd be home free. Not even five minutes behind schedule.

Kyle looked both ways and began pedaling, flying down the hill to regain momentum. The icy air bit at his face, and he blinked against the wind blowing into his eyes as he coasted to the bottom. He saw a black pickup that had paused for a moment at a stop sign. He was pretty sure the driver hadn't seen him. Better to stop and be sure.

Kyle slammed on his brakes.

He felt his bike shudder.

And then everything went dark.

***

Sam slid into the driver's seat of his truck and smiled. The job had taken longer than he had anticipated, but his client had been thrilled with the extra care and attention that he'd been able to provide. He'd even asked for his business card so that he could recommend Sam to his brother who had just fired the electrician working on his halfway-completed house. More business, more connections. It was a good start to the day.

He twisted his key in the ignition and heard the engine roar to life. A quiet chime played next to him, and he reached for his phone. A number he didn't recognize had left a voicemail. Probably another job. He'd call them once he'd finished driving.

He had a few missed texts from Kyle. Sam opened the messages. Ahhhh...right. The game. He'd forgotten. But it looked like Kyle had taken matters into his own hands and figured it out. *Good for him.* At least he hadn't called Nicole. He dropped the phone into his cup holder.

Sam shifted into drive and began to pull away from the curb when his phone rang. He glanced down at the screen. Odd. It was the same number that had left the voicemail. Whoever was calling obviously wanted to get ahold of him, so he put the truck back into park and picked up his phone. He slid his thumb over the slidebar to answer. "Hi, this is Sam with Frontier Electric."

"Hi Mr. Richardson, are you the father of Kyle Richardson?"

A wave of dread washed over him, and Sam froze. "I...I...yeah, Kyle's my son. Who's this?"

"This is Officer Jason Kendrick with Devon Falls PD." The man's voice was steady but kind. "I'm sorry, sir, but your son was in a bike accident this morning around 10:30 on Morningside Drive. He is on his way to Valley Memorial right now."

Sam's vision tipped, and he felt for the seat beneath him. His fingers gripped the cold leather and squeezed. Anything to keep him steady. "Is he...is he...what happened?" His brain was misfiring. Language was a chore.

"Your son is alive, but he is injured. You were his last attempted call." The officer paused. "Sir, you need to go to the hospital as soon as possible."

"Of course, I'm on my way right now." Sam took a deep breath. His heart was pounding so hard that it felt like it might jump out of his chest. His hands shook as he shifted his truck into drive and squealed away from the sidewalk. "What happened? How bad is he hurt?"

"I'm sorry, sir. Those are questions that you'll need to ask the doctors at the hospital. I don't know any specifics."

Sam swallowed. "Okay. Thanks." He hung up the call and dropped his phone onto the seat beside him in a daze. The hospital was ten minutes away, and he swore in frustration. It was too long. What if he couldn't make it in time and something happened?

No. He couldn't think about that. Sam shook his head to clear it. He had to get to the hospital and...

Nicole.

He needed to tell his wife.

Sam picked up his phone again and hit Nicole's contact. It rang four times before she picked up. "Hey, how's the game?'

"Game?" His mind was blank. All he could think about was Kyle alone in an ambulance.

"Kyle's game. Are they winning?"

"Nicole, I need you to listen to me." Nausea churned his stomach, and he rolled through a stop sign before slamming his foot back to the gas. "Kyle's been in an accident. He's on his way to Memorial, and I'm heading there now."

After a beat of silence on the other end, her voice turned panicked. "Wait, what? What are you talking about?"

"I just got a call from the police. Kyle was in an accident this morning."

"What do you mean you got a call? Aren't you with him?"

Sam gripped his steering wheel as if it were a lifeline. "No. I got held up at work."

Silence.

When Nicole finally spoke, her voice was low. "Did he get hurt at the game?"

Sam gritted his teeth, guilt crashing over him. "No. He was on his bike, and it sounds like it happened on his way there."

More silence.

"I'll be there in fifteen minutes." He had never heard her sound so cold toward him. And he knew he deserved every ounce of it. The call disconnected without a word of goodbye.

Sam raced down the highway, the needle of his speedometer hovering close to eighty. Guilt settled like a blanket, smothering him. He gasped for air, terror and regret sitting heavy in his chest. *What if his injuries are lifelong? What if he dies?* Scenario after horrible scenario flashed through his mind and he choked, tears burning his eyes. What in the world would he do without Kyle?

This is my fault. Entirely and completely his fault.

When was the last time the two of them had even spent any time together? Aside from a passing joke or an irregular family dinner, they both lived fairly separate lives with Sam's long hours, Kyle's school and sports practice all day, and then friends and homework in the evenings. Sam racked his brain. What was Kyle even into? What did he like?

A recent memory replayed in his mind. Kyle had mentioned liking the Millers' entryway. There had been a cross displayed in it. Was Kyle more interested in faith than Tyler? Did he read his Bible? *Why don't I know this?* He'd never thought to ask. He had just assumed everything was fine and that if Kyle had questions, he'd come talk to him.

Nicole's voice echoed in his brain. *Something's off, Sam.* This is what she'd meant. Somehow, in the midst of their busy life, he had stopped knowing his son.

The hospital was five minutes away now, and Sam blinked rapidly to dispel the moisture in his eyes.

Nicole was right. Something needed to change.

***

Nicole clung to Abby's hand as she crossed the hospital parking lot, desperation thick in her chest. She needed to see Kyle. Needed to know he was all right. She reminded herself to breathe as they walked quickly through the sliding double doors and into the emergency department.

A twenty-something redhead at the admissions desk disentangled her headset from her hair. She saw them approach and smiled. "Hi. Can I help you?"

"My son..." Nicole heard her voice shake and cleared her throat. "My son was just brought here in an ambulance. His name is Kyle Richardson." Her eyes dipped and read the girl's name badge. *Sarah K., ED Desk.*

"Richardson..." Sarah's fingers flew over the computer's keyboard, and she frowned. "I don't have him in my system yet. Was this recent?

"Yes, I just got the call about fifteen minutes ago."

"Okay, he's either still on his way or so new to the ED that he hasn't been put into the computer." She motioned to the waiting room. "If you want to have a seat, I can send someone to go check for you."

There was no way she was sitting down. "He should be here already. Please, I need to find him."

"Nicole!"

"Daddy!"

Abby pulled away from her, and Nicole spun at the sound of her name. Sam pushed his way through the inner doors of the emergency room and waved her to him, scooping Abby into his arms and scrunching her dance costume against him. "Hey, kiddo." His arms were like vice grips around her middle. Nicole could tell how badly he didn't want to let her go.

Sam looked at Sarah in explanation. "This is my wife and daughter. My son was just brought in." He reached out a hand and beckoned to Nicole. "He's okay so far. They just finished assessing him, and he's awake."

Sarah handed Nicole a clipboard with a pen attached. "Feel free to go with your husband. We will just need his information when you have a chance so we can put him in the system."

Nicole thanked Sarah and rushed to Sam, heart hammering in her throat. Was it possible to feel this many emotions at once? Relief. Terror. Gratitude.

And fury. So much fury.

Sam led her through a hallway of open individual rooms. They passed by a teenage boy getting stitches, a toddler covered in hives who was screaming at a nurse, and a janitor changing the sheets of a rolling bed. The rest of the rooms were empty. They rounded a corner into another hallway. Nicole swallowed. "How bad is he?"

Sam grabbed her hand and squeezed, his other arm still tightly wrapped around Abby. "He has a broken leg and a concussion. He's going to need surgery on his leg. They're prepping him now."

It could have been so much worse. But a concussion? That was unnerving. "How did you get back here?"

"I literally got here the same time as the ambulance. They let me walk in with him." He took a left and the hall dead-ended at a cluster of rooms. "Where's Hannah?"

"She was about to go onstage when I got your call, and I couldn't pull her from the dance. I'll pick her up at Kara's. Did they tell you what happened?"

Sam paused outside of room 116. "It looks like he was riding down Morningside and hit black ice. He crashed into a truck that was stopped at a stop sign and flew over the hood." He set Abby gently onto the floor. "His leg got tangled in his bike, and he wasn't wearing his helmet."

"What? Why not?" The kids always wore their helmets. It was something that Sam had drilled into all of them.

Sam set his mouth in a hard line. "He said it was cold, and he wanted a beanie. He couldn't wear both." He looked at Nicole, a pleading look on his face, and said in a low voice, "I know this is my fault."

The fight was completely out of him, and Nicole felt herself soften for a moment before anger coursed through her veins. She wanted to scream at him. He had no right to look so dejected when she hadn't had the chance to let him have it. Nicole blinked away angry tears and shook her head. "I don't want to talk about that right now. I want to see my son."

"I'll stay out here with Abby." Sam pushed open the door to the hospital room, and Nicole brushed past him. Kyle was lying in the bed, surgical cap perched cockeyed on his head. A bruise was swelling purple at his right temple, scratches etching a pattern down the side of his face to his chin. His left leg was stabilized and elevated, but at an unnatural angle. Nicole's breath caught in her throat, and she almost tripped as she rushed to Kyle's side, her fingers clutching his hand.

"Ouch. Hey, Mom."

"Hi, honey." Tears trickled down her cheeks, and she wiped them away. "How are you feeling?"

"I've been better."

"I bet." Nicole gently brushed his hair off his forehead. His skin was cool to the touch. "Dad said you have to have surgery on your leg?"

Kyle grimaced. "Yeah, they're supposed to come and get me any second."

She wanted to comfort him but wasn't sure how. "I'm sure it will go completely fine, but if you're scared, that's okay." Kyle had never had surgery before, and he was hard to read. He could be terrified, and Nicole doubted she would know.

He gave her a bemused expression. "I'm fine, Mom. Honestly, what I hate the most right now is this thing." He held up an arm and showed her the IV attached to the back of his hand. "So annoying."

Nicole's eyes darted to another bruise on his elbow.

"Oh, that. Good thing I had my coat on. Pretty sure it's the reason my arm isn't ripped up."

She wanted to strangle Sam. Instead, she gestured to the surgical cap he was wearing. "How's the head?"

"I was kind of hoping to get amnesia but so far, no luck. Just a lousy headache."

Nicole felt a laugh bubble up in her chest, and she wiped at her eyes. "Well, I see one thing that escaped unhurt was your humor."

Kyle flashed her a half grin. "Always."

He was quiet for a moment, and she watched a shadow pass over his face. His eyes turned serious.

"Mom." Kyle's throat worked, and he swallowed. "I'm really sorry about all this."

She heard the door squeak and turned around to see a nurse's blonde head pop through the opening. "Mrs. Richardson, we're ready to take Kyle to surgery now, but your husband wanted to make sure you got a couple more minutes with him if you wanted."

She didn't want to hold up the surgery. "I'll be out in just a minute." The door clicked shut, and Nicole gently kissed Kyle's forehead. "This wasn't your fault, okay? I don't want you blaming yourself. You just focus on healing. You didn't do anything wrong."

Kyle shook his head. "No one made me choose a cap over a helmet. That was just dumb." He paused and watched her face. "Maybe it's not anyone's fault, Mom. Sometimes accidents just happen."

The fact that he refused to blame his father made Nicole equally proud and irritated. Sam didn't deserve Kyle's protection when Kyle was the one lying in a hospital bed and minutes away from an operation directly caused by his dad's irresponsibility. Uncertainty curled in her stomach. It also bothered her that Kyle hadn't thought to call her cell and ask for a ride when Sam hadn't come home. She wanted to know why. She wasn't like Sam; she always showed up. So why hadn't he called?

But this wasn't the time to talk about any of that.

Nicole forced a smile. "You're right, sometimes they do." *This just isn't one of those times.* If Sam had made his family a priority, none of them would be here right now. "We'll be waiting here when you're out of surgery, okay? We're not going anywhere. I'm going to get your nurse." She gave his hand one last squeeze and headed for the door.

"Mom?"

"Yes?

There was a beat of silence and then Kyle said quietly, "Don't blame Dad, okay?"

* * *

"Are you going to eat?"

Sam was looking at Nicole with concern as she walked back to her chair in the waiting room with a third cup of coffee in her hands. It tasted terrible, but it was hot, and she was desperate to dispel the chill that emanated from within her own body. Her hands shook ever so slightly, and her fingertips seemed unable to get warm. She wasn't sure what was causing the trembling: nerves, adrenaline, caffeine? Maybe all three. It didn't help that all she'd eaten that day was an apple on her way to the dance competition at 7:30 this morning. Now it was almost 1:00, and the lunch hour was almost over. But if she was hungry, her stomach didn't know it. She mostly felt electrified: on edge and jumpy.

"I don't think I can eat anything right now."

Sam glanced at Abby, her legs lounging over the arms of a chair in a corner. She was listening to an audiobook on her tablet, earphones in, a bag of Doritos from the snack machine half-eaten in her lap. Sam stood up and walked over to her, quietly asked a question, and then took the Doritos. He held them out to Nicole when he sat down. "Eat these."

"I'm not taking her food."

"She's all done, I asked. Otherwise, I was going to buy you something from the vending machine." He pushed the bag into her hand. "You have to eat something, even if you don't feel like it. What have you had today?"

"An apple."

Sam let out an exasperated sigh and tapped the bag. "Eat."

Obediently, Nicole stuck a couple of fingers into the plastic and pulled out one nacho flavored tortilla chip. It was not appealing. She ate it anyway.

Sam watched her for several seconds, then leaned forward and rested his elbows on his knees. He laced his fingers together and clenched them tight. "Okay. Let's have it out."

Don't blame Dad, okay? Kyle's words echoed in her memory. He might as well have asked her to fly. "What am I supposed to say, Sam?" Her eyes flickered to Abby, still absorbed in her book. She kept her voice low. "'I told you so' seems a bit petty but then again, our son is in surgery because you couldn't be bothered to think about anyone other than your-self." She reached for another chip. "Every time I've asked you to work less or make time to connect with the kids, you've brushed me off and said we're fine when I know we're not." She clenched her jaw. "But apparently it took one of our children cheating death to make you think that maybe I might have something legitimate to say." She shot a glare at him. "So yes, I did tell you. And yes, I think this is your fault."

It was good that they were in a public space. If they'd been at home, they would probably have escalated to a yelling match. Then again, maybe that was why Sam wanted to talk about it here and now.

Sam stared at his hands. Silence stretched between them. And then...

"Everything you just said is completely true." He rubbed the back of his neck and looked at her. She'd never seen such a tortured expression on her husband's face. "I have dismissed you because I thought you were overreacting. But the truth is, I realized on my drive over here that I don't even know much about Kyle anymore. And that can only be true if I really have been absent."

Nicole stared at him. Part of her was thrilled that he had finally had this epiphany. The other part wanted to scream, *Why couldn't you have figured this out yesterday?*

"Do you know what he told me when I got to talk to him?" Sam pinched the bridge of his nose. "He told me that he wasn't surprised that I didn't come because he knew how much work needed me." He shook his head. "They don't, Nic. But he thinks they do because the alternative is to believe that his dad picks work over his family." He swallowed. "That's never what I meant to do."

That she completely believed. "I know you never meant for it to come across that way. I just wish you'd believed me when I told you that it did." Nicole pulled the last few chips free from the bag. "I just don't understand why he didn't call *me*." She put one into her mouth and bit down. "I wasn't far away, and I could have come." That feeling of unease crept back into her stomach. Did he think she was as unreliable as Sam? That made zero sense.

A small groan escaped Sam's lips. "Oh, he told me why."

"He did?" Nicole was shocked. "Did he just forget?"

"Nope." Sam sat back in his chair and grimaced. "He said he knew that if he called you, you'd know I didn't show up and be mad. And he didn't want us yelling at each other again."

It was as though a bomb of clarity had detonated between them. Nicole stared at the empty Doritos bag, the reality of his words hitting her squarely in the face.

How many times had the two of them ended the evening with raised voices, Sam disappearing into the basement to escape her yelling at him and herself sleeping alone with a pillow soaked with angry tears? She'd thought the kids were fairly oblivious to their marital struggles, too focused on their own activities and entertainment to pay attention to the tension between their parents. But evidently, her son had decided not to call her for help because he didn't trust her to handle it in an emotionally healthy way. She looked at Abby tucked into her corner of the waiting room. What burdens were their eight-year-old carrying that they had foolishly assumed she was too young to notice?

She was not blameless in this after all.

Nicole clenched the bag and crushed it into a ball. She felt tears sting her eyes, and her hands started to shake again. "This is my fault too."

Sam reached out a hand and covered hers with his. "I'm more to blame than you are, but I'm going to say something that you've said to me multiple times lately. Something needs to change." He stared hard at her face. "I mean it, Nic. I get it."

Nicole felt her hands still. She took a deep breath. "Do you mean that?"

"I do." He squeezed her hand. "I want you to get in touch with the Millers."

"Why, because Tom works in medicine?"

"No. I want to do that parenting class."

Nicole blinked. "What?"

"Call them. Have them sign us up or whatever we have to do." Footsteps echoed down the hallway in their direction and Sam stood up as Kyle's surgeon entered the waiting room. "Text her, Nicole. I'm serious."

The surgeon pulled his facemask down and revealed a smile as he approached. "Kyle's surgery went extremely well, and you can see him when you're ready, though he'll probably sleep for another half hour or so."

A warm wave of relief swept over Nicole, and her shoulders sagged. She had no idea she'd been holding such tension in her shoulders. *Good news. Finally.*

"Thank you so much for taking care of our son." Sam stretched out a hand and shook the doctor's.

"Getting back on his feet is going to take some time because of the severity of the break, but I expect him to make a full recovery." The surgeon's eyes darted between the two of them. "Do you have any questions for me?"

Nicole shook her head. All she cared about was that Kyle was going to be fine. *Thank you, Lord.* The prayer slipped into her mind and nearly surprised her. She realized that in the midst of the panic, she had forgotten to pray until now. All her focus had been on Sam.

Guilt twisted, and she winced inwardly. Blaming instead of praying. Even if her frustrations were valid, this was not a great strategy.

Nicole stood up and walked to the trash as the surgeon beckoned them to follow him down the hallway. She tossed the crumpled plastic bag into the bin and turned to see Sam in the corner with Abby. She watched as he tenderly pulled the earbuds out of her ears and stuck her tablet back into her backpack. He zipped the outside unicorn pocket shut and took her hand.

"Come on, baby girl. Let's go see your brother."

CHAPTER 5

Nicole unzipped Kyle's backpack and lifted his Chromebook out of the padded pocket. "Okay, which textbooks am I giving you first?"

Kyle sat back in his wheelchair, leg propped up on a neighboring stool, his fingers fumbling with the wad of cords dangling from his school laptop. "Math and History."

The golf clubhouse was almost deserted. Only hardcore golfers were interested in trekking the greens when the temperatures were low, but Tom had insisted that this was ideal for their first parenting class meet-up.

Well, calling it a class was generous. When Nicole had called Jessica to explain Sam's sudden change of heart, Jessica had explained that they had two options: An online video course or one-on-one mentorship with a family who had already been through the program. The church only did the class once every other year, and as Nicole felt time was of the essence, she and Sam had opted for the mentor relationship. The Millers had graciously agreed to be their mentor family, delighting Nicole.

Their plan was to hit the golf course for a round of nine, then meet back up at the clubhouse for supper. Kyle couldn't join them for obvious reasons, but he'd missed school for almost a week and had a chunk of homework to attack while the rest of them were out. Nicole glanced out the window at the dreary sky outside. The wind whipped the American flag at the clubhouse door, and she shivered. She half-envied her son's ability to stay inside.

"They're here!" Abby beamed and skipped to Kyle's table, her cheeks rosy. "I just saw their car."

"You can go out and say hi, if you'd like," Nicole said, handing Kyle his binder and pencil pouch. "Do you need anything else?"

"Just the novel in there. This should keep me occupied for a couple of hours." Kyle sighed and flipped open to a blank piece of paper. "If I'm dead when you come back, blame Algebra 2."

"You're not allowed to joke about being dead for at least eighteen months." Nicole tapped his arm with *Frankenstein* and placed the book on top of his impressive stack of assignments. "Enjoy your cheerful book. I hated that one."

Kyle gave her a wicked grin. "If you love me, you can write my chapter summaries."

"You'd fail. It's been over twenty years, and technically I only read the cliffnotes when it was assigned to me." Nicole ruffled his hair and smiled. "Don't get any ideas."

Kyle gave her a sarcastic salute. "Yes, ma'am."

The doors of the clubhouse opened, and Nicole could hear Abby chattering happily at Whitney as the Millers filed into the main room. Nicole pointed to the counter. "The guy over there is named Jeff, and he said if you need anything, just ask. They're super slow today."

"See if they'll give me one of those little summoning bells."

Nicole laughed and squeezed his shoulder. "You'd be a monster."

Jessica made her way toward them with a cheerful wave, a wide smile on her face. "How's the invalid?" She motioned to his leg. "Has most of the pain passed?"

"For the most part. He's still in excellent spirits, all things considered." Nicole gave Jessica a quick hug and returned her smile. "Though he's currently bemoaning the pile of homework that has accumulated for him over the past week."

"So would you, if you were me." Kyle tapped *Frankenstein* on top of his homework pile and grimaced.

"Ahhhh," Jessica said, picking up the book and flipping it over. "I won't lie. I hated this one."

Kyle let out a huff. "Okay, between you and my mom, I am seriously dreading this thing."

Nicole suppressed a laugh. "It builds character, honey."

"Go golf."

Jessica laughed. "You have a point. We probably should get on the course if we want to be finished before supper." She turned her attention to Nicole. "Are you good with the teams we picked?"

Nicole nodded. With eight of them golfing, the families were going to pair off and then split up. Tom and Wyatt would golf with Sam and Tyler, who had come home for the weekend to see his brother. Jessica and Nicole would team up with Whitney and Will, who was cast-free and ready to do something two-handed. Hannah had never golfed before and wasn't interested in making a fool of herself in front of other people, and Abby was too young, so the two of them were content to ride in the golf cart for fun. Nicole silently prayed that Hannah would be kind to her sister. Hours in the cold and a moody preteen were not exactly a good recipe for sisterly peace.

They decided to skip the driving range, and within ten minutes, all of them were out on the course. Nicole and Jessica had encouraged the four guys to start first, as they were more competitive and interested in finishing all nine holes. Once they'd collected their golf balls and repositioned the flags, the moms and teens got started. Jessica hung back with Nicole while Whitney teed off.

"So, is Kyle doing as well as he seems?"

Nicole nodded. "He really is. He's always been a happy-go-lucky type of personality and tends to roll with things. This is no different. He was even cracking jokes when he woke up from surgery."

Jessica laughed. "So, is he the family clown?"

"More so than anyone else, I'd say." Nicole pulled a driver out of the golf bag she'd rented and wagged it in Jessica's direction. "Be warned. This is going to be highly comical."

"No judgment." Jessica peered at the club. "At least you picked the right one."

Whitney stepped aside after taking her shot, and Will stepped into position. Jessica lifted her own driver out of her bag. "Does Sam enjoy his humor?"

Nicole shrugged. "He tolerates it. Sometimes Kyle really gets him laughing, but they don't spend a ton of time together."

"I know you mentioned over the phone that Sam's been working a lot of overtime, and it's brought some strain on your family. Is he having trouble connecting with the kids?"

Nicole laughed. "I don't think I can say he has trouble when he just doesn't try in the first place." She felt a twinge of guilt. "Well, that's not totally fair. He's trying, which is why we're here, and I'm thankful for that."

Jessica's brow creased in curiosity. "Has it always been this way or was he more involved when the kids were little?"

Nicole thought for a moment. "He was more involved, but mostly with the boys. Especially Tyler." She sighed. "That's a sore subject, actually. He's always been way more interested in Tyler than the other kids, and it has bothered me for quite a while."

Jessica watched Will tee off. "Have you ever talked to him about it?"

"Yes. In his defense, it's not like he's the one who can hang around the ballet studio or backstage at all the competitions. A lot of them are during his working hours. But he rarely comes to their recitals or asks about what they're doing. And Kyle—" Nicole shook her head. "Kyle isn't Tyler."

"What do you mean by that?" Jessica gestured to the tee markers. "And you're up."

Nicole stifled a moan and walked over to get into position. It had been years since she'd golfed, probably before Abby was born. She and Sam used to go a lot when they were dating, but once they gotten married and the kids had come along, it hadn't been a priority for her. "Just be warned, this is Sam's sport, not mine."

"What's your sport?"

"Reading." Nicole swung her driver. The ball went flying down the fairway. It didn't go as far as Whitney and Will's, but it was generally in the right direction, so it could have been worse. "At least I hit it."

"That you did," Jessica said.

Nicole stepped back and waited for Jessica to finish their group. Her ball made a beautiful arc and landed farther than anyone else's.

Nicole smiled. "Sam said you were good."

"High-school muscle memory, that's all." Jessica jammed her driver back into her golf bag and the four of them made their way down the fairway. "You said this is Sam's sport. Do any of the kids play with him?"

Nicole shook her head. "Sam uses the golf course to relax. I think bringing a child or two with him would defeat that purpose in his mind." She shrugged. "He did take Tyler back when he was around Abby's age, but it didn't last long. It was kind of a way for the two of them to get out of the house and do something when Kyle and Hannah were still little and needed to nap." She squinted, remembering. "I think he took Kyle once for his birthday, and he's never taken the girls."

Jessica cocked her head thoughtfully. "So, he's made efforts with Tyler that he hasn't with the other kids?" Her face softened. "I'm not judging him. I'm just making sure that I'm accurately understanding your perspective on his relationships with them."

Nicole let out a frustrated sigh. "It's not just my perspective. It's the facts. Sam has always made time for Tyler. I think it's easy for him because they're so much alike." She ticked a list off on her fingers. "They're both into sports, they have similar humor, and they choose a lot of the same activities when they have down time. Even when Sam has worked a lot, the two of them have found time to connect because they'll want to sit down and watch the same movie or go throw a football to unwind. Their relationship is easy." She felt her chest tighten slightly. "The rest of us take more effort for him. Kyle is funny and relational, but he isn't the sports superstar that Tyler is, which is fine. But you're more likely to find him out with a group of friends or on his computer." She grimaced. "Especially now because he's officially out of sports till next fall."

"Is Sam not into those things?"

"Computer games?" Nicole laughed. "No, definitely not. I mean, he does have friends and enjoys being with them, but he works so much that he doesn't really get together with anyone." She gestured to the course around them. "Unless they're up for golfing."

They were coming up on Nicole's ball, and she began rummaging in her golf bag. "Okay, which one should I use?"

"Do you have a fairway wood?"

"It's sweet that you think I know what that is."

Jessica grinned and peered at her clubs. "Hmm. I think you just have irons in here, so that one." She tapped the one etched with a *3*. "I'm guessing the girls don't spend a lot of the time with their dad either?"

Nicole pulled the iron free and rested her hand on the handle. "No. Hannah spends a lot of time at the dance studio, and Abby usually tags along. Sam would rather endure torture than sit through a weekend

Nicole felt a twinge of annoyance. *Orlando.* With Kyle's accident, it had slipped her mind. Sam almost always missed Heritage's Christmas program because it fell the same week. She hated that trip.

Instead, she forced a smile and flipped over her menu to look for their list of hot beverages. "We didn't keep score either," Nicole said. "But I'm pretty sure I would have been the biggest loser." Tea. That sounded perfect. "I am curious though. What's the connection between parenting and golf?"

"Isn't it obvious? Parents are the irons; kids are the balls. You whack us till we go in the right direction," Kyle said. There was a beat of silence, and then everybody burst out laughing.

Tom wiped his eyes on his sleeve. "We should have Kyle teach this, just for entertainment's sake."

"I would be excellent," Kyle said, gesturing to the table. "I'm already at the head, just like King Arthur."

"King Arthur's table was *round*, Kyle. This is an oval," Hannah said with a giggle.

"Ovals are round."

"Circular, I mean."

Kyle shrugged. "Potato, potahto."

Tom held up a hand. "Okay, question for all of you who golfed." He glanced at Nicole and nodded. "I promise this is answering your question. I can't speak for your group, but we had a variety of skill levels in ours. Sam was, as already established, excellent. Wyatt and Tyler were decent. I proved that I'm basically the court jester for King Kyle over there with how badly I played." He gave a slight bow and there was another round of chuckles. "So how about Will and the ladies?"

"Like I said, we didn't keep score," Nicole said, interested to see where Tom was going with this question. "Jessica was usually done first, then Whitney and Will. I was always last and lost two balls."

Abby leaned into her mother's shoulder. "I think you did a good job."

"Thank you, sweet girl." Nicole smiled. "Anyway, we obviously had different skill levels too."

Tom nodded. "And why do all of us have different skill levels?"

Sam answered this time. "Some of us like golf more than others, and not everyone regularly visits the course. I mean, I've worked hard on my game the past several months and I've definitely seen an improvement that I wouldn't expect to see if I played only a few times a year."

"Yeah, my game has tanked," Tyler said, nodding in agreement. "I've only golfed a couple times this year so I'm obviously not getting any better."

Nicole shook her head and said, "I golfed some in my twenties but that's it."

"Now, she reads," Jessica said with a wink. "As for me, I golfed a lot in high school and was pretty good. I go maybe once a month, but mostly for fun. Sometimes Tom comes with me, but it isn't his favorite activity, so he hasn't spent a lot of time playing."

A waitress appeared with a notepad and the next few minutes were spent ordering drinks, perusing the menus, and promising to be ready to order by the time she returned a second time. Nicole ordered peppermint tea and unzipped her coat. She was finally warming up.

Tom ordered last—a large Dr. Pepper—and turned his attention back to the table. "Golf has a different level of priority for everyone at this table. That priority isn't stagnant either. It can change." He looked at Nicole. "You said you golfed fairly often in your twenties and then stopped. What changed?"

Nicole glanced at Sam. "We got married and both worked full-time. Plus, golf is expensive, and it wasn't in the budget in those early years. Then the kids came along, and it just wasn't something I cared about enough to make it a focus of my life again."

"So for you, golf has lessened in priority as your life circumstances changed where for Sam, it's increased," Tom aid. "This is an illustration of the first point I want to make in our discussion, which is the importance of seeking God."

Sam raised an eyebrow. "I'm having a hard time seeing the connection."

Tom held up a finger. "It will crystalize, I promise." He took a sip of water. "The most important aspect of parenting is your relationship with God, and I'm not just talking about having a daily individual quiet time, though that is certainly important. Worship should also be the foundation of your marriage and your family life with your kids." He folded his hands and lowered his voice slightly. "How would you two say you're doing in that department?"

Nicole felt something inside of her squirm. This was getting uncomfortable, fast. She glanced at Sam and saw his expression tighten. "Um," Nicole offered, trying to ease the sudden tension she was feeling. "I don't read my Bible and pray as much as I should. I certainly don't have time set aside every day to do it."

Sam nodded. "Same. And we've never thought to do it together." He shot a look at Nicole. "At least, I haven't."

"Neither have I," Nicole said.

Tom smiled encouragingly. "Remember, this isn't a time for you guys to feel embarrassed or like we're judging you. We've been there." Tom pointed at Jessica. "I know this can be uncomfortable, but we're on your team. We really want you to believe that."

Sam's expression eased, and Nicole breathed a sigh of relief. Sam motioned to the kids sitting around the table and said, "As for the kids, that's the reason we enrolled them at Heritage. We wanted them to have a Christian education that would prepare them for life and be based in Scripture." He sat up a little straighter. "We haven't been to church much lately, but they go to youth group. At least they did when we were attending Breakthrough. Personally, I feel like we've done a good job with that part."

"Okay," Tom said, sitting back in his chair. "Nicole, do you agree with that assessment?"

"Some," Nicole said. "Sam's not wrong. We have made Christian education a priority for our kids. But we don't sit down and study God's Word together as a family or anything. We don't go to church a lot and even though the older kids go to youth group—" Nicole wrinkled her nose. "I think they mostly play games and hang out. There doesn't seem to be a lot of teaching going on."

"That's true," Kyle said. "Youth group is mostly a giant playdate for teenagers."

"Anyway," Nicole said, not looking at Sam. "I feel like we've mostly left their spiritual development up to the school and any church attendance we've fit in."

Sam looked at her in confusion. "That's literally their job."

The waitress was back, a tray full of various drinks perched expertly in one hand. Nicole accepted her tea gratefully and breathed in the steam. Ahhh. That was better. The conversation stalled as they went round the table and ordered, burgers and sandwiches by far the most popular items for their group. Nicole chose fish tacos and a side salad, then ordered a cheeseburger for Abby with a side of fries and a fruit cup. Listening to all their selections made her hungry, and Nicole found herself hoping that due to the emptiness of the clubhouse, their meals would be delivered quickly.

Tom thanked the waitress and drummed his fingers on the table. "Okay, let's bring this full circle." He turned to Sam. "Why would you say you're so good at golf?"

An easy question. "I'm in a golf league."

"But it's more than that. How does that affect your game?"

"I make sure to be on the course often, and my buddies and I give each other pointers." He snapped his fingers. "Oh, and this summer we hired a private coach for a month to help us improve our total average."

"So, you put a lot of time and energy into being a good golfer," Tom said.

"For sure."

"Tyler," Tom said.

Tyler was mid-conversation with Wyatt but looked up and said, "Yeah?"

"Why weren't you happy with your golf game today?" Tom asked.

"Oh, I wasn't upset."

Tom waved his hand in the air. "I know you weren't, but you didn't play as well as you used to a few years ago, right?"

"Right.

"Why not?"

"I'm way out of practice," Tyler said, looking at his dad. "Which is totally fine since I had to choose between sports in high school, but it did mean I stopped golfing regularly. I lost any edge I had when I was younger."

Tom pointed at Nicole, then at her husband and son. "What are you hearing them say about their golf games?"

Nicole could see the direction he was going. "Sam is good because he puts the time and effort into the sport and even gets some coaching, while Tyler is out of practice, coachless, and hasn't spent much time honing his skills." She grinned at her son on the other side of Sam. "No offense, bud."

"None taken. I mean, I can't be amazing at everything," he teased.

"Jess, you want to explain the point I'm trying to make?" Tom reached his arm behind his wife and squeezed her shoulder.

Jessica smiled. "The same observations that Nicole just made about golf can be applied to your family's spiritual life and your parenting journey as well. Sam didn't become a great golfer by accident. Similarly, a strong family isn't built without focused commitment to God and His Word." She tucked a strand of hair behind her ear. "Reading your Bibles regularly and discussing what you're reading, praying together, keeping each other accountable in your church attendance, these are all practices that will 'firm up your game,' so to speak."

"If these things aren't prioritized, our faith weakens," Tom said. "Like Tyler's golf game, ignoring them will cause you to stagnate or go backward. It takes hard work and effort, but they will make a big difference in the health of your soul and your family."

"They're called spiritual disciplines for a reason," Jessica said. "Sam has tremendous discipline as a golfer and has surrounded himself with a league to help him improve even more. The same is true of the Christian life. It's important to surround yourself with like-minded believers who will spur you on in your faith and family life. Listening to podcasts and reading good books by reliable authors can be really great resources too."

Sam looked thoughtful. "I feel like we surround our kids with a lot of good things already with youth group and school." He looked at Kyle. "Maybe not youth group."

"Not every youth group operates like Breakthrough's," Jessica said. "You guys are more than welcome to try out Grace's. I think it's on the same night."

"I'd like to try that, actually," Kyle looked at his parents. "I'm serious. I have fun at Breakthrough, but lately it's seemed kind of pointless, and

I'd like to try out one that's more into studying the Bible." He tapped the wheels of his chair. "Hope you guys don't have stairs."

"Not too many," Tom grinned.

"See?" Sam gestured in Kyle's direction as if he proved his point. "Christian school, a good youth group, and a renewed commitment to go to church." Sam nodded to Nicole. "I really do feel like that's a lot we're doing."

"It is a lot," Tom said. "But the question is, how much of it are *you* actually doing?"

Sam cocked an eyebrow. "I don't follow."

Tom folded his hands. "I want to reemphasize that there is no judgment here. I know that some of these things are hard to hear, so please know that we aren't trying to criticize you or make you feel bad. We're in a unique position in this conversation because you've asked us to mentor you through this process, and that means that things will sometimes be uncomfortable or tense." He gentled his voice. "From what I can see, you have your kids in a lot of Christian environments, and that's good. But it sounds like you're exclusively outsourcing their spiritual development." He held up his hands. "Don't get me wrong. Heritage is a great school, and Grace is a great church if you start attending there, but your kids are only getting spiritually fed from those two sources. If I'm wrong, please tell me."

Sam and Nicole were quiet. He wasn't wrong, and Nicole felt her stomach tighten with unease.

Sam cleared his throat. "I guess I've always just believed that's the job of the church and school. I provide for my family, and I work hard, but I'm not a Bible scholar or a teacher."

"You don't have to be," Tom said. "The truth is: a lot of parents make this assumption. What we've noticed is that families who rely on other places—good places—to provide their kids with biblical knowledge often find themselves in two common pitfalls." He held up one finger. "First, some kids leave home and lose all interest in spiritual things if it isn't built into their lives. They were passive in their faith and never made it their own. They quickly become enamored with the world and often leave the church entirely."

Nicole stared hard at her napkin, determined not to look directly at Tyler. She chanced a glance out of the corner of her eye and saw that he was looking at Tom with rapt attention.

Tom held up a second finger. "The second pitfall is more subtle and has to do with compartmentalizing one's faith. I know a lot of kids who have gone through a Christian school and were raised in church who still lack the ability to think through life with a biblical worldview. They're Christians," Tom said, "but when faced with difficult situations at work or at home, they don't always know how to think biblically about day-to-day life. They have great doctrine, but they don't know how to bring it home. Teaching our kids how to do that is a huge part of parenting."

A wave of panic rose in Nicole. How in the world were they supposed to do that?

Jessica offered Nicole a smile across the table. "Are you okay?"

"I just..." Nicole rubbed her eyes and stifled a groan. "This just seems really overwhelming."

"This is something that we learn as we go," Jessica said. "And it's one reason why your own spiritual walk is so vital to parenting. You can't give what you don't have. But if you're faithfully reading and praying and learning a little each day, you will be amazed at how much you grow in your understanding and faith. God gives us the grace we need."

Tom looked at her intently—and then grinned. "This is a marathon, not a sprint. It's about daily obedience, not perfection. And remember, it's the Lord doing the work in you. You're not alone in this." He glanced behind him. "Let's get back to this in a few minutes, I think our food is coming."

He was correct. To everyone's delight, the kitchen was fast and efficient and had gotten every order right. Ketchup bottles were passed along the table, samples of fries and onion rings were swapped, and Nicole discovered that she loved red-pepper aioli when it was drizzled over lightly battered fish. Eventually, Tom pulled out a manila folder from under his chair and passed a copy to anyone who wanted to follow along as he talked.

"These are mostly for you two," he said to Sam and Nicole, "but your kids are welcome to read through this as well so they can get acquainted with what you're trying to establish in your home." He tapped the document. "It's easy to remember because it's just one word."

Nicole's eyes darted over the piece of paper. It was simple. The top showed an outline with the word ADEPT written out in an acrostic with various Scripture references on each line:

A - Attentive (Psalm 103:13, 1 Peter 5:3, 1 Timothy 3:4, Luke 15: 11-32)

D - Discipline (Proverbs 13:24, Proverbs 19:18, Hebrews 12:6)

E - Encourage (Mark 10:14, Colossians 3:21, 1 Thessalonians 5:11)

P - Provide (1 Timothy 5:8)

T - Teach (Proverbs 22:6, Deuteronomy 6: 5-9, Deuteronomy 4: 9-10, Deuteronomy 11:19, Psalm 78: 2-4, Ephesians 6:4)

Tom picked up his copy and pointed to the first line. "This is actually part of your homework, but I want to walk through this with you really quick to make sure you don't have any questions. In ADEPT, A stands for attentive. Parenting requires us to pay careful attention to our kids with purpose and care." He moved his finger down the list. "D is for discipline. A lot of parents today think that loving their children means allowing them to act however they wish because they need to express themselves.

This is foolishness. Raising children requires discipline—self-discipline for the parents and instructional discipline for the kids."

Nicole nodded. They'd always been fairly consistent with discipline, and she was grateful for that. Being attentive was harder, especially for Sam. They were so busy...

"E is for encourage," Jessica said. "This one is so important as our kids grow and change. We don't only need to encourage them in their academics and activities, but in their character development and spiritual lives as well."

"P is for provide," Tom said, glancing at Sam. "As guys, it's easy for us to focus on the material aspect of provision because it takes up so much of our lives. But we also have to provide emotional support and instruction to our kids. Provision isn't only about meeting physical needs."

"And last is T for teach," Jessica said. "Sam, I know you've mentioned a few times that this is the job of the school and the church, but the Bible actually places the primary responsibility of teaching on parents, especially fathers."

There was a beat of silence, and then Nicole asked the question whose answer scared her. "Does that mean we have to homeschool?"

Jessica laughed. "No, not at all. Homeschooling can be a great option for families, but it isn't the only one."

"But if we're supposed to be the ones teaching our kids, how does that work without homeschooling?"

Tom sat back in his chair. "Parents are commanded to give their kids a Bible-centered education in Deuteronomy 6 and Ephesians 6. That doesn't mean that they have to be the instructors of every single subject, but it does mean that it is the parents' responsibility to ensure that such an education is taking place and that they are actively participating in it. Does that make sense?" He looked at Nicole. "To put it simply: there's a big difference between parents who put their kids in a Christian school but never have spiritual conversations at home, and ones who send their kids to the same school and have a family life defined by worshiping together at church and having spiritual conversations at home."

It made sense. It was also a lot.

"As heads of our homes, the bulk of this responsibility rests on dads," Tom said. "And this is something that even the world has recognized. Children with spiritually active dads are more likely to stay in the faith than if only Mom is involved."

"That's true," Kyle said, dipping a half-eaten fry in ketchup. "I had to do a survey project on that subject last year, and I found like, three different studies that all said the same thing." He popped the fry in his mouth and looked thoughtful. "And honestly, it's pretty true of a lot of my friends. Ezra, Jamison, and Levi are more committed to church and stuff than anyone else in my group. Ezra's dad is a pastor, and Jamison's dad is really involved with all his kids. I see him around a lot."

"What about Levi's dad?" Nicole asked.

"His parents are divorced, but he hangs out with his grandpa a lot, and he's the one who brings him to church and pays for his school tuition. Maybe they have a father-son thing going on."

Nicole peered around Sam at Tyler. "Would you say that's true of your friends at college?

"Uhhh," Tyler said, giving his mother a guilty look. "Honestly, none of my friends are very religious, at least not that I can tell."

Well, that certainly explained why he wasn't being encouraged to attend church or stay away from drinking. Nicole stifled a sigh. She wished Tyler would seek out some new friends. Though a college campus probably wasn't the best place to find a wealth of spiritual maturity.

"Okay." Sam swallowed a bite of his cheeseburger and looked at Nicole. "I think we are both committed to trying some of these things out." He looked apprehensive, but Nicole saw him set his jaw, a sure sign of determination. "I'll be honest: we probably won't be able to do everything you guys do, but we'd like to do some of them."

Tom grinned. "The bottom of your paper should help with that. I listed off some habits that many families have incorporated into their lives while they're doing this course. The goal is to jumpstart and then maintain Christ-centeredness in your home."

Nicole skimmed the list at the bottom of the page. The habits seemed so basic. And yet, virtually none of them were a regular practice in their home. Shame curled in her stomach. She felt like such a hypocrite.

- *Weekly corporate worship at church as a family*
- *Daily individual Bible reading and prayer*
- *Weekly praying/discussing reading as a couple*
- *Family worship at home: Sing, Read, Pray (3-5 times per week)*
- *Daily family and/or individual spiritual conversations with children*
- *Scheduled family fun*

"Attending church as a family is vital to the Christian life, so that one's at the top of the list. And then of course, it's important that both parents are reading their Bibles and praying each day." Tom put his finger on number three. "This one is often skipped, but we personally recommend it. It's easy to keep our spiritual lives private when we're married, but there is a strength and blessing that comes when parents spend time in the Word and pray together. It produces a unity that is truly unique and is also a great time to discuss what you're each reading and learning in your Bibles."

"What exactly do you mean by family worship?" Nicole asked. "Is this like having devotions together?" They'd done that when the kids were small.

"Devotions can certainly be a part of it. Family worship is simply a time that you all gather as a family and sing a song, read, and discuss a chapter of the Bible, and then pray together," Tom said. "When our kids were young, it was short—maybe five to ten minutes. Now that they're older, we tend to go deeper in our discussions. We take Sundays off since we're in church and usually there's another day that we miss it, but our goal is five days a week." He offered a smile. "We usually suggest starting out with three days a week at the beginning, with a goal of increasing to five once you find your rhythm." He took a long drink of Dr. Pepper. "The next one can look different depending on the day. The goal is to have some sort of spiritual conversation with each of your kids each day. You can do it around the dinner table all together, you can do it with just the girls or just the guys, you can do it one-on-one." Tom listed off their options. "There's no right or wrong way. This forces you to practice talking about deeper things with your kids so that it becomes a natural part of your relationship."

"And if you're stumped for ideas, asking your kids what they're learning in Bible class or in their own reading is an easy springboard," Jessica added.

Nicole slipped a pen out of her purse and wrote down the advice. *Ask kids what they're reading/learning about the Bible.* Her eyes hovered over the final item on the list. *Scheduled family fun.* Like a vacation? Their last one had been such a disappointment.

Sam held up a fry covered in ranch and pointed it at Tom. "I won't lie. I'm a little nervous about how we're going to fit all of this into our schedule."

"Give it some time. It will get easier," Tom said.

"I'd actually like to hear from your kids," Nicole said, sticking the pen back into her purse. "I want to know how they've seen these habits be helpful in their own lives, and maybe some of the things they've enjoyed doing for fun as a family?"

Tom surveyed the table and the younger faces on either side of him. "Okay, Millerites, do me a favor?" He raised his voice slightly to get their attention. "I want you each to tell me one way our spiritual practices at home have helped you apply your faith to your life, and one specific thing we've done that was fun and memorable."

"I'll go first," Whitney volunteered, looking up from a makeshift game of tic-tac-toe she was playing with Abby on the back of one of the papers. "Middle school was a really hard time for me. I was struggling a lot, and that meant I wasn't always very nice to my brothers."

Will raised his hand. "That's how I got my first broken arm."

Everyone laughed, including Whitney.

"I wasn't *that* mean. But my parents brought me back to the Bible again and again, and they prayed with me and counseled me through the issues I was having. I learned a lot during that time." She made a face at Will, and he made one back. "And as for a fun memory, my favorite has always been Surprise Nights."

"What's that?" Abby made an X through the final tic-tac-toe box. "Cat's Game again."

"Surprise Nights start at 5:00 and go till late," Will said from the other end of the table. "We never know when they're coming, which is how they got their name. We'd sit down for dinner and under our plates would be a list of everything we were doing that night. Usually, we'd go out to eat and then do something fun, like mini-golf or a movie or go-karts. Then we'd end up back home and eat banana splits and play board games."

"None of the things we did were particularly exciting, but the surprise was the fun part," Jessica said.

Wyatt raised a hand. "I always liked when we did overnights with Dad or Mom. It was just twenty-four hours away at a hotel somewhere, but we'd go spend some time together one-on-one and find something fun to do close by." He thought for a moment. "I'd say that the spiritual routines have been really helpful now that I've moved out on my own. I keep doing what we've always done, but now I do them by myself. I think it would be a lot harder to try and establish something like that if I'd never experienced it before."

Will looked down the table and nodded toward Tom. "I don't rely on my friends the same way that a lot of kids my age do. I'm really close with my parents, especially my dad, and I'd much rather talk to him about deep stuff and get his perspective on things because I know he takes the Bible seriously and loves me enough to tell me the truth." He raised his eyebrows. "Plus, most thirteen-year-olds are just dumb." Will paused as a ripple of chuckles went round the table. He pushed away his empty plate. "I'm not being mean. It's true. Anyway, my favorite fun thing is the Journey to Bethlehem event we do every Christmas."

Tom looked at Sam and Nicole. "Does that help?"

It did.

"Ready for your homework?" Tom handed them each a three by five card with a small list of to-dos written on it. "The first assignment is to look up each of the verses at the top of that paper I gave you and see what the Bible teaches about each of the ADEPT steps. The second part is to set some goals for yourself in your spiritual disciplines and try to meet them this week." He tapped the paper. "This list is a goal, not a starting point. We want you to feel free to start slowly so that you don't get overwhelmed.

And last, we want you to talk with each of your kids about some things they'd like to do with you for fun."

It was a starting point. Nicole ran a hand through Abby's curls. "I think that sounds doable."

Sam nodded. "It does."

Tom turned to Sam. "Remember, you get to be the lead on this, but if you have any questions or need to talk something over, I'm available." He cocked his head toward his wife. "And so is Jess if Nicole wants to chat. When you guys have it all done, let us know, and we can set up session two."

LESSON 1:

Seek God – Learn to be more A.D.E.P.T. (Attentive, Discipline, Encourage, Provide, Teach) parents as you spend more time in God's word individually and as a family.

CHAPTER 6

"**O**oooo, what are we doing?"

Abby spoke for all of them as the Richardsons walked into one of Grace Fellowship's adult classrooms on the first Saturday in December. A foldable red and blue gymnastics mat lay about a third of the way across the width of the room, while two others lay several feet away from it in opposite, diagonal directions, almost as if each one was set at the point of a triangle.

"Looks like a game, honey," Nicole said, glancing at Sam. He was smiling. He loved games and competition.

Tom and Wyatt were across the room setting up a round table in the corner for Kyle, who had graduated to crutches but still couldn't participate in any physical activity.

"Hey!" Wyatt said, grinning as he unfolded a padded chair. "The crutches look good! How's it feel to be vertical?"

"Taller." Kyle crossed the room without trouble. Hannah trailed behind him with his backpack as the rest of the family unzipped their coats and piled them against one of the walls. "And the pain is pretty much gone unless I have to do physical therapy."

"That's good," Tom said. "Thanks, Hannah." Tom took the bag from her and swung it onto the table. "Still catching up on homework?"

"Nah, just getting ready for midterms. I was at a study group before this."

Tyler joined them at the table and grasped Wyatt's hand. "Good to see you, man."

"You too."

Tom turned his head as the door opened again and the rest of the Miller family came hurrying in from the cold. "They beat you, slackers!" Tom called. He winked at Hannah as she giggled.

Jessica unwound the scarf around her neck and gave Nicole a quick hug as she stacked their jackets into their own family pile. "They were eating cake when I got there. I had to give him a couple extra minutes!"

"Will was at a birthday party," Tom said. "They were picking him up on the way here and *promised* me they wouldn't be late."

"Technically, I think we were just early," Jessica said, glancing at her watch. Three on the dot.

Whitney and Will walked over to the table while Jessica and Nicole brought up the rear. Nicole smiled as the kids all greeted each other. They had passed the awkward getting-to-know-you phase and seemed to be becoming friends. She wondered if having Kyle and Hannah try Grace's youth group this week had helped that along.

Tom waited until the conversation lulled, then turned his attention to Sam. "Okay, so Thanksgiving is over, and the Christmas festivities are revving up, but you guys still managed to get your homework done. So, well done! How did it go?"

Sam stuck his hands into his jeans pockets. "We think it went pretty well." He looked at Nicole, and she nodded in agreement. "We sat down as a family one evening and talked about different ways that we can add some of those spiritual routines into our family. We think we came up with some good goals." He cleared his throat. "It's been kind of tough. Our schedule is full, but we have definitely made an effort."

Tom gave them an encouraging smile. "That's totally fine. We're playing the long game here. Immediate results are ones that probably won't last. Slow and steady is much better."

Nicole felt herself relax. She had been worried that a less-than-perfect first week would earn them a you-can-do-better speech.

"You guys are going to figure out what works for your unique family through trial and error," Jessica said. "Honestly, it took us a long time to get a rhythm down in our home, and we still tweak things now and then because people grow and change. That's just life."

Abby raised her hand and bounced up on the balls of her feet.

"The cute one has a question," Tom said.

Abby smiled, ponytail bobbing, and pointed at the gym mats lying on the floor. "Are we playing a game?"

"We are!" Tom rolled up his sleeves and rested his hands on the table. "It's called Crossing the River. Have you guys played it before?"

"No," Nicole said, looking at the rest of her family. They were all shaking their heads.

"Excellent, neither have we. Except Wyatt, that is." He pointed at his son. "He played it at camp one summer for a team building exercise, so he's actually going to explain it."

Wyatt took off his baseball cap and ran a hand through his hair before promptly replacing it. "The goal of Crossing the River is to get from one side of the room to the other without touching the floor. The floor is a river that's so dangerous and poisonous, that if you touch it with any part of your body, you'll die."

Hannah cocked her head to the side. "So, it's like Floor Is Lava?"

"Without any cool props, yes." Wyatt pointed at the three mats. "So, the mats are islands, and these are rocks." He picked up two large, green carpet squares. "You guys get two of them. And then each of you gets a stepping stone." He pointed to another pile of smaller, orange carpet squares.

"This'll be easy," Hannah said with a grin.

"Ahhhh, not so fast. There are some ground rules." Wyatt pointed to the green squares. "You get two rocks to place wherever you'd like, but once they've gone into the river, they can't be moved. Neither can the islands."

Tyler crossed his arms. "There goes my plan to launch myself at a mat and pretend it's a raft."

"What about the stepping stones? Can they be moved?" Nicole asked.

"A stepping stone can be moved, but only by the person who puts it down."

"So, if Nic puts hers down, only she can pick it up to put it somewhere else?" Sam asked.

"Correct."

"Last of all," Wyatt said, "your entire family has to step out of the river at the same time. This means no one can do all the work and make a path, and then everyone else just follows. You're in this together, and you have to finish together." He grinned. "I promise it's harder than it sounds. Any questions?"

Tyler put up a hand. "Are piggybacks allowed?" He winked at Abby.

"Completely allowed," Wyatt said.

"Can someone put down more than one stepping stone?" Sam asked.

Wyatt shook his head. "You each own a stone that's yours. No delegating."

Hannah pointed at the orange squares. "You said we can move our stones, but how are we supposed to not touch the floor with our fingers when we pick them up?"

Wyatt nodded. "That circumstance is the only one that allows you to technically touch the floor. Good question."

"Can I provide strategy assistance from the side?" Kyle asked.

"Totally."

There was a moment of quiet. Tom clapped his hands. "Okay! Looks like you guys have all the info you need. We'll provide rule reminders if you need them. Otherwise, try to cross to the other side in ten minutes."

Nicole picked up five orange squares and two green, then followed Sam and the kids to one side of the room. It seemed pretty simple. She certainly didn't think they'd need ten whole minutes to accomplish the task. She passed out the orange carpet squares and set the two green ones on the ground.

"And...the game starts...now!" Tom pushed the timer on his phone and sat down next to Kyle.

All five of them stood still, waiting.

"Don't all try at once," Kyle called from his place at the table.

Nicole cleared her throat. "Um...should we put a rock down first or a stepping stone?" The first mat was several feet away.

Abby stepped forward and gently laid her orange square right in front of her.

"Stop it!" Hannah shrieked, pulling Abby back. "What's that supposed to do?"

"It's a stepping stone!"

"Yeah, to nowhere!" Hannah pointed at the square. "Pick it up."

"No! I like it there."

Sam pinched the bridge of his nose. "Abby, sweetie, can you pick up your square please? We're going to need to put it somewhere else."

Crestfallen, Abby picked it up.

Tyler grabbed both green squares and threw one of them a few feet in front of him, then took a running leap and landed in the middle of it. He grinned. "Who's next?"

"I don't think anyone but Dad can make that jump." Nicole gauged the distance and shook her head. "Could you both even fit on the mat?"

"Nice going, genius," Kyle laughed. "You forgot your stepping stone, and it's too far for you to jump to the island."

He was right. When he'd picked up the green squares, Tyler had left his orange one behind.

"Ooookaaay." Tyler looked behind him and then back at his family. "Yeah, I'm stuck. Who wants to come to my rescue?"

"You don't need to be rescued," Sam said. "We just need to get you a stepping stone. Can we bring him his stone?"

Wyatt nodded. "As long as you don't use it."

Sam flung his own stepping stone onto the ground and hopped onto it, the forgotten square tucked under his arm. He tossed it to his son, and Tyler caught it. "My hero!" Tyler swooned.

The girls laughed from the wall.

Tyler tossed his stepping stone onto the ground. It sailed farther than he meant to, but not so far that he couldn't reach it. With a long leap, he set one foot onto the orange carpet square, then launched himself forward onto the first gym mat. "Alright, one down and two to go."

"You can't finish without us!" Hannah reminded him.

Sam hopped onto the green square and looked back at Nicole and the girls. "You ladies coming?"

Nicole nodded to Abby. "You go first."

Abby wrinkled her nose. "It's too far."

"It's not..." Nicole's voice trailed off. Abby was right. It was a fine distance for Hannah, but Abby's legs weren't long enough to make the jump. "Okay, put your square down right there, and then use that to hop onto the other one." She pointed at each of the carpet pieces on the ground. "So, you'll go like this: orange, orange, green, orange, island. Sound good?"

The words were barely out of her mouth when Hannah went flying through the air onto the orange square, landing neatly in the middle. "Ha!"

"It was my turn!" Abby said, indignant.

Hannah looked at her smugly. "Too slow, Baby Sis."

Abby opened her mouth to retort, and Nicole held up a finger. "Stop." She turned to Hannah. "If we're obviously working on getting her over, you need to cooperate. That was obnoxious."

Hannah looked over at the Miller family and turned bright red.

Nicole motioned to Abby. "Go ahead and put your square down."

Abby placed her square a couple feet in front of her and hopped onto it.

Now they were all in a line: Abby and Hannah on orange stepping stones, Sam on the green rock, and Tyler on island number one. "Okay, all we have to do is this all over again to get to the next gym mat."

Sam joined Tyler on the island, and Hannah followed. The gym mat was getting crowded. Abby hopped onto the next orange square, then the green. Nicole stepped onto the first square, feeling slightly silly.

"Hannah, put your stone here so we can get to the next island." Tyler pointed to the floor a few feet in front of him. The second mat was only a few feet away. Hannah put her square onto the ground and Tyler skipped onto it, then tumbled onto island number two.

"Are you okay?" Nicole watched Abby frown at the orange mat lying between her spot on the green square and the first island.

"It's too far again!"

"We can use my stone. Just a second." Nicole jumped onto the green square and swayed. She and Abby were almost on top of each other. She tossed her stone forward, and it landed two feet away.

"Dude, what are you *doing*?" Kyle's voice broke her concentration, and Nicole glanced up. At first, she didn't know why he was asking the question, but then she realized that Tyler had just put down the other green square in a place that didn't make any sense.

Tyler looked up at his brother. "Uhhh, making a path?"

"Why are you going to the third island? You can get to the wall from there if you play it right!"

"We have to go to the third island first."

"No, you don't. That wasn't in the rules."

Tyler looked at the Millers. "Don't we have to hit all three islands?"

Wyatt shook his head. "Sorry, man. You just have to get to the wall."

Hannah let out a groan. "You wasted our last rock! Now all we have are the stones!"

Nicole looked behind her. They could probably get Abby and Sam's stones back since they didn't need them anymore. She tugged her daughter's shirtsleeve. "Abby, can you go back and get your stepping stone?"

"I'll try."

Abby hopped back onto Sam's square, then crouched, her fingers grasping for her own. "I can't reach it!"

She couldn't.

They were officially down a stepping stone.

"Hang on, I can get mine." Sam leapt from the first island and then to the orange squares. He stared at Nicole, who was still perched on the green carpet like a seagull. "Babe, I don't think we'll both fit."

Probably not, but they needed the stones.

Sam did his best to jump from Tyler's square to the place Nicole was standing. One foot landed on the square. The other hit the floor.

"DAAAADDDDDDDDDDDDDYYYYY!" Abby wailed, hands covering her face as she shrieked. "DADDY'S DEAD!"

Everyone burst out laughing.

"Sorry Sam, you're out," Tom told him.

Sam waved a hand in Abby's direction. "It's okay, Abs. Just promise you'll visit my grave."

"I CAN'T. THE RIVER IS POISON!"

Kyle shrugged. "She makes a fair point."

Abby hopped back to Nicole's side, then made her way to the first island. Nicole jumped to her own square then to Tyler's. She reached back to grab hers and just managed to scoop it up with her fingers. Two stones and a rock were officially out of play. They'd need this one for sure. She stepped onto the first island and joined Abby.

"Everyone please note that Mom outlasted Dad in this river-of-the-zombie-apocalypse scenario," Kyle said.

"Excuse me." Sam seated himself on Kyle's other side and elbowed him in the ribs. "I gave my life to try and help you people. Give me some credit."

Nicole took note of their predicament. Tyler might be able to get his stepping stone back now that she and Abby had made it to the first island. Nicole was the only one with a stone, which wasn't enough to finish. She waved to Tyler. "We're gonna need your stepping stone!"

"On it!" Tyler made his way back to the first island, hopping carpet squares like an expert.

"Can you reach it?"

"Can I reach it," Tyler scoffed, kneeling on the mat and reaching out for his stone. "Where's your confidence in me, Mom?"

"It's over on the second green rock with mine!" Hannah reminded him.

Tyler managed to loop his fingers under the carpet and pulled it back. "Got it." He began to make his way back to the second island.

"Wait! Tyler, hold on," Nicole called him back. "Can you piggyback Abby—"

"And...time's up!" Tom hit the button on his phone.

Already? How was that possible?

"Epic failure," Kyle said.

Sam laughed.

"Told you it was harder than it looked," Wyatt said, walking across the room and picking up the carpet squares. "You should have seen some of the teams at camp when we did it. It was hysterical."

"We were close," Hannah said. "If we'd had like, ninety more seconds we totally would have made it."

"Technically you lost a team member so you would have lost anyway," Wyatt said.

"Poor Daddy," Abby said, running to throw her arms around Sam. "I'm sorry you died!"

Sam tapped her on the nose. "Good to know I'll be missed."

"Okay, it's our turn." Tom held up his phone. "Who wants to time us?"

"Me!" Hannah raised her hand.

"Perfect." Tom handed her his phone and grinned. "No cheating."

"I don't cheat!" Hannah laughed.

"Hey, wait," Tyler said as the Millers began to walk to the other side of the room. "How is this fair? Wyatt's done it before!"

"I'm only here as an extra body," Wyatt said. "They get to tell me what to do, and I don't get to give any input. Scout's honor."

"You guys ready?" Hannah held the phone in one hand and looked at them expectantly. They all nodded. "Okay...go!"

Nicole watched as Tom pulled Jessica and the kids into a small huddle, pointing at various places on the floor and very obviously coming up with a plan of attack. Whitney shook her head and held up her orange square. Nicole tried to hear what they were saying, but the huddle muffled their voices. She could only understand bits and pieces.

"...and then you..."

"...but I can jump to the green..."

"That's good, but Mom needs to move..."

"...and then I can go to that one."

Two solid minutes passed before Tom held up a hand. He was ticking items off on his fingers, pointing at each person, and then pointing at the floor. Another minute passed. The entire family nodded.

Sam leaned back in his chair. "They just used up a third of their time on a plan."

Nicole wrinkled their brow. "Smart. We should have done that."

He arched a brow. "A plan's no good if you don't have time to execute it."

"Yeah, but it prevents people from putting rocks where they don't belong," Kyle said. Tyler punched him on the arm.

Tom clapped Will on the shoulder and handed him one of the green squares. "Okay, you put this as far as you can jump and still make it without trouble."

Will threw down their first green mat and hopped easily onto it, then tossed his own orange square onto the floor in front of him but didn't move to it.

"Okay, Whit. You go," Tom said. "Just make sure you don't put yours too far for Will to reach his." Whitney jumped to green and then to Will's square, adding her own stepping stone in front of his. She stepped onto it, then leaped to the first island. Jessica and Wyatt followed the same path, and last came Tom. Soon, the four of them all stood squashed together on the first island, and only Will was still on the green mat. Tom threw his orange square onto the ground and hopped off the first island onto it.

Hannah frowned. "What's he doing?"

"I think he's making sure Will has enough room to stand on the island," Nicole said.

Will grinned and hopped to Whitney's square, turned around and picked up his own, then jumped to the island. Whitney knelt on the side of the gym mat and reached across the floor, scooping up her square.

Abby's eyes were wide. "They're all on the island, *and* they all have their stepping stones!"

"All they have to do is basically repeat that process," Tyler said.

It was true. Nicole watched as Tom swapped places with Jessica. Jessica laid her stepping stone in front of his, then hopped to the second island. The kids all followed, Wyatt bringing up the rear. Tom jumped to his own orange mat, then Jessica's, turned around to pick his up, and joined everyone on the island. Whitney set her stone on the ground and hopped onto it to make room for her dad.

"They have one rock and all five stepping stones left," Hannah said. "They're really good."

Tom took the final green mat and threw it in front of island number two. Nicole watched with interest. He still couldn't jump from the rock to the wall; it was too far. Tom tapped Wyatt on the shoulder. "You first. Make sure you only go as far as you know you can jump."

Wyatt leapt onto the rock and then—to Nicole's surprise—threw his orange mat at an angle. He jumped onto the mat and waited. Whitney was next, aiming her own square fairly close to Wyatt's and hopping on. Will tossed his own directly in front of the green mat.

"Ahhhh," Sam said. "They're getting in position. See how Will has the clearest shot? He's the shortest so he needs the smallest distance."

He was right. Jessica and Tom laid out their stepping stones on Will's other side and soon, all five Millers were in a straight line on their orange squares. "On three," Tom instructed. "One, two, three!"

They all jumped into the air, landing safely on the so-called riverbank.

Hannah stopped the timer. She raised her eyebrows when she looked at the time.

"How long did it take us?" Jessica asked, eyes bright.

"Your total time was six minutes and eight seconds," Hannah said. "That's crazy!"

Kyle drummed his knuckles on the table. "Sickening, really."

Sam ran a hand through his hair. "I won't lie. That was seriously impressive. Though I still protest because you got to watch us go first and make all the mistakes."

Jessica laughed. "Fair point."

Tom gestured for the rest of them to sit, and they pulled up a few more chairs. The table wasn't big enough for all of them, and they ended up in a crooked oval. Tom held up his hands. "I admit: we did have a couple pointers from the curriculum that pointed us in a helpful direction. It recommends starting with a group huddle to come up with a strategy."

Hannah gave him a mocking shocked expression. "You *cheated*!"

"It's not cheating if it's in the teacher's guide," Tom said, chuckling. "Hannah, you tell me. Why would starting with a huddle be a good idea?"

"So that everyone knows what the plan is and what they need to do to get to the goal," she said.

"Exactly."

"And so no one puts rocks in dumb places."

Tyler rolled his eyes. "Touché."

"Was there anything else we did that would have helped the way you guys approached the task?" Jessica asked.

Nicole put up a hand. "You had a leader."

"That was another pointer they gave us: Have one person be the instructor." Tom looked at Abby. "Why do you think that's a good idea, Abby?"

Abby wrapped a curl around her finger. "Because it's confusing if you have two people telling you what to do."

"That's right. And they might even tell you opposite things."

"You guys stuck together really well," Sam said, his gaze flickering to Tyler. "No man left behind."

Tyler looked sheepish. "Yeeeaaah, sorry. I was trying to find a good path to hit all three islands and got too far ahead."

Tom looked over at him. "Okay, that's interesting. You had a specific goal that you took upon yourself to help your family get across. But—" Tom waved his hand at the rest of the Richardsons. "—did any of you realize what he was doing?"

"No. Otherwise we would have told him he didn't need to include all three islands," Kyle said.

Tom nodded. "A worthy goal can be a hindrance to your family if the rest of your people aren't on board with it."

"Or even aware of it," Hannah said.

Jessica raised a hand. "I'm curious who each of you were looking to as the leader. Was there one person who you assumed was calling the shots?"

Everyone talked at once. A chorus of, "Tyler," "Sam," "Me," and "Mom," echoed in the room.

Kyle's mouth turned up at the edges, and he leaned over to talk to Whitney. "It explains so much."

She swallowed a laugh.

"Let's take a poll," Tom said. "Hannah, you first."

Hannah looked at her oldest brother. "I was following Tyler."

Sam raised his hand. "Me too."

Tyler nodded.

Nicole shook her head. "Not me. I was watching Sam."

Abby leaned against her mother. "I just did what Mom said."

Tom leaned forward and rested his elbows on his knees. "It looks like because you guys didn't have an established leader or goal, you were looking to different people and trying to do different things." He looked at

Tyler. "Let's see how this translates. You had a great season last year on the football team. How would your year have gone if your team didn't have a leader or a specific goal in mind?"

"Uhhh...we would never have made it to the championships."

"Why not?"

"It's hard enough to be a good team when you have those things." He looked at Wyatt. "I mean, a lot of teams are really good and have great coaches, and they still never make it that far. A team completely without them would bomb, no question."

"You were the star player. Couldn't you have carried them?"

"No, it's a team sport." A knowing smile crossed his face. "Yeah, okay. I get it."

Sam ruffled his son's hair. "You're such a superstar, man."

Tom grinned. "The title of today's session is 'Target or Trajectory.'" He looked at Abby. "I bet you know what a target is, but do you know what a trajectory is?"

Abby shook her head.

"Trajectory is the path that an arrow takes on its way to a target," Tom said. "If I shoot an arrow into the air, its trajectory is up. If I shoot it at the ground, the trajectory is down."

Abby wrinkled her brow. "So, it's the way it goes?"

"Basically." Tom turned his attention to the rest of them. "Knowing where your target is will determine the trajectory you choose for your arrow. If my target is on the wall, it makes zero sense for me to fire my arrow in the direction of the door and expect to hit the bullseye."

It made sense. Nicole just wasn't sure what they were supposed to do with the metaphor. "Are you saying we need a shared goal? One the whole family is aimed at?"

"A shared purpose is probably closer to what I was thinking, but yes." Tom sat back in his chair. "To have a shared purpose, everyone needs to know what the purpose is and be aiming toward it. If multiple people have different goals, you'll end up at cross-purposes, which is a recipe for conflict."

"Let's use us as an example," Jessica said, looking at the confused looks on their faces. "When we went through this class, Tom and I had very different ideas about how we wanted our family life to go. I grew up doing a lot of sports and activities, and so I wanted our kids to have those same experiences because I loved them. Tom grew up on a farm and didn't do a ton of those things because he always worked. We started arguing as the kids got into school because I'd want to enroll them in any activity I could, but he didn't like them being so busy and gone in the evenings when they were little."

"Going through this class helped us realize that one of the reasons that we had such different goals is because we didn't have an overall purpose we were aiming at," Tom said. "We sat down one night and talked a lot about what we wanted for our family. I'm talking big-picture stuff. We both wanted our kids to love the Lord deeply, and we wanted our home to be centered on Scripture and honoring Christ. We also wanted to have a connected family life that would prepare and launch our kids into life as capable adults. Once we figured that out, we were able to sort through how we were both processing the kids' activities. I realized that if I wanted my kids to be proficient in multiple things, I needed to give them opportunities to explore their strengths and hobbies. That stuff takes time."

"And I realized that one of the reasons I was able to do so much as a kid was because I was an only child," Jessica said. "That kind of schedule wasn't sustainable with three children if my bigger desire was for us to have a connected family that actually spent good time together." Jessica cupped her cheek in her palm. "We both adjusted, but the adjustments were pointed in the same direction rather than different ones."

"Sounds like you guys compromised," Sam said.

"We did that too," Jessica said.

"Your homework for this week is going to be similar to what Jess just explained," Tom said. "Like a strong team has a leader and a common goal, we want you guys to come up with something similar." He grinned at Tom. "Congrats on being Dad. You're the leader."

Sam winked and slid an arm around Nicole's shoulders. "Excellent."

Tom laughed. "Don't misunderstand me. Nicole is a big part of this too. A smart team is united in purpose, but they also know the strengths and weaknesses of the members. Usually Mom is the one who has her finger on the pulse of her people, and her insights and opinions are massively important."

Nicole smiled.

Tom looked at Tyler. "I assume there's a reason you played wide receiver, but not kicker all through high school."

Tyler snorted. "Our kicker was just the top soccer player in a football uniform."

"But he could kick better than you."

"Totally."

"There you go." Tom motioned to Tyler, as if he'd made his point. "One reason Tyler did well on his team is because he was playing the position that fit his strengths and not one that didn't. The same goes for families. Understanding the people in your home, their unique personalities and struggles, their preferences and talents, this knowledge can help you navigate situations and make choices that fit your particular family. As parents, it's really important that you work as a partnership in this."

Nicole was grasping. "Can you give us an example?"

Jessica jumped in. "One spring, we had Will sit out of baseball. Obviously, we love the sport, and Wyatt had been playing since he was little, so we didn't have any problems with the time commitment. But they got a new coach who switched practices from Tuesdays to Wednesday nights. On Wednesdays, our kids were already involved in a Bible club at church that they really loved, and we didn't feel comfortable having him skip it for several weeks. Will was also super shy and had been working to connect with some of the kids his own age at church and had finally gotten close to a couple of boys. We didn't want to jeopardize that. One of our big family values is actively training our kids in the faith, so we told him we were going to take a year off. He was bummed—"

"Still am," Will said.

"—but we're glad we made the choice we did," Jessica concluded with a smile. "And in this case, it ended up working out. We weren't the only people who pulled their kids that year. The coach ended up switching the night back to Tuesdays the next spring because of the low turnout." She shrugged. "Most of the time it doesn't button up so nicely, but I remember being really thankful that he could play the next year."

Sam squeezed Nicole's shoulder. "So, our homework is to come up with some kind of family purpose statement?"

Tom held up a few fingers. "Two things. First, a family purpose statement. Second, a list of your family values."

"Wait, how is that different than a purpose statement?" Kyle asked.

"The purpose statement is the overarching vision that you want for your family," Tom said. "The little booklet we sent home with you last week has some examples if you need some inspiration."

"Your family values should be things that you want to define your family," Jessica said. "Basically, they're your priorities and ideals that directly point you to your purpose statement."

"So, the purpose statement is the target and the values are the trajectory," Sam said.

"Exactly."

Nicole felt herself squirm. "That sounds like something a business would do," she said. "I'm not trying to be difficult. This just seems kind of forced." *And honestly, a little weird.*

"I totally get it. I felt the same way when we went through this. I thought it was strange," Jessica said. "What I didn't expect was that as weird as I felt about it, it was actually really clarifying. Tom and I were missing each other and didn't even know it."

"Think about your great-grandkids," Tom said. "What would you want them to inherit from your family, legacy-wise? A good work ethic? A commitment to their family?" He folded his hands. "Or you can be morbid and think about how you want your kids to talk about their childhoods at your funeral."

Kyle began a eulogy. "Once, my dad couldn't stand on a green carpet square and fell to his death into a poisonous river...."

A round of laughter echoed off the walls.

Tom stood up and brushed the back of his jeans. "Let's hope we all die before Kyle so he can give commentary at our memorial services." He beckoned them all to follow him. "Any questions or can we get onto our big activity of the day?"

"You said to wear good walking shoes, so I assume we're going to be on our feet?" Nicole asked.

"Yes, ma'am."

The families exited the classroom and walked down the church hallway. It curved to the left and dead-ended at another door next to a set of bathrooms.

"Here we are," Tom said, leading them into the church kitchen. Food was everywhere. "Your family gets to work as a team tonight. This big window opens into our fellowship hall, where they're expecting two hundred people from the community for dinner tonight. We get to serve them." He saw their panicked faces and laughed. "Don't worry. It's not as hard as it sounds, and we're here to help. We have the side dishes and desserts already, and the main dish is being catered." He turned to Sam. "You five are going to be the serving team. It's up to you to pick out who does what, but you'll need three of you to serve food, one pouring drinks, and two keeping the tables clear."

"We'll mostly be keeping the food coming," Jessica said. "But if things get crazy, you can always grab one of us. And let us know if you run out of anything so we can replenish the serving dishes."

Sam pulled his family aside as the Millers got to work pulling salads out of the fridge and opening boxes of cookies. "Kyle, are you good with pouring the drinks? I think it's the only job that will keep you off your feet."

Kyle nodded. "Can I set up a drink table on the other side of the window? That will leave more room for the food, and it will be easier for me to get up and use my crutches if I need to."

"Do that. That's perfect." Sam looked at Tyler. "Can you set him up?"

"Sure."

"Nic, can you be one of the servers? You'll have a good idea of portion sizes. So will Tyler."

Nicole nodded. "Yep."

"Can I be with Mom too?" Hannah asked. "I want to serve the desserts."

"That's fine." Sam looked at Abby. "What do you say, kiddo? You want to be my table-clearing assistant?"

Abby beamed. "Can we have pie afterward?"

"Probably."

"Yes!"

***

"I'm beat," Sam flopped onto their bed and let out a sigh. He glanced at his watch. "At 8:07. Pretty sure this is a new personal low."

Nicole laughed from the bathroom, a toothbrush halfway to her mouth. "How many tables did you put away?"

"Too many." He stretched his back and grimaced. "Those things must have been secretly made of granite. They were so heavy."

"Or you're getting old."

"You're two years behind me, baby. If I'm old, so are you."

Nicole could see his feet hanging off the bed in the reflection of the bathroom mirror. "Take your shoes off before you lose the ability to sit up, Grandpa."

Sam kicked off his shoes and pulled himself farther onto the bed. "What time is church again?"

"Sunday School starts at 8:30. Service is at 9:45."

"Okay." Sam sat up with a groan and shrugged out of his sweater. "Then I need to be up by 7:15."

Nicole rinsed her mouth in the bathroom and placed her toothbrush back on its charger. She reached up to unfasten her earrings. "Abby looked like she was having fun with you tonight."

"We had a really good time," Sam said, his hands starting to work the buttons on his collared shirt. "All the old people loved her. She was doing cartwheels for them by the end of the night."

"Oh yes, I saw that." Nicole smiled. "One of the ladies told her she used to do back handsprings when she was little, and Abby was very impressed." She walked the earrings over to her jewelry box in the closet. "Was she actually helpful cleaning up though?"

"Oh, yeah. She did better than I thought she would, as a matter of fact." Sam stood up and joined her in the bathroom, tossing his shirt in the hamper. "I had her stack all the paper plates together and then the plasticware on top. Made it easy for me to come along and scoop things into the trash."

"Cute." Nicole took the sweater he'd slung over his shoulder and reached into the closet for a hanger. "You realize she didn't need to stack stuff though, since everything was disposable."

"I know, but I thought it was a good habit to teach her. You used to wait tables. You know how nice it is when people halfway clean-up for the bussers."

Something warm bloomed in her stomach, and Nicole's heart skipped a beat. He'd thought about teaching Abby kindness and responsibility, even when it wasn't necessary. She swallowed. "I really love that you did that."

Sam looked at her, a bemused expression on his face. "Why?"

She nudged his shoulder. "Because you taught her a way to bless other people and go the extra mile, even when you didn't need to." Something she'd read last week in Ephesians tickled the back of her mind. "I respect that."

Sam raised his eyebrows. "Seriously?"

"Seriously."

"Hmm." Sam grabbed his toothbrush and stuck the head on the shared base. "Did you have a good time?"

"I did." It surprised her how true the statement was. "You know, I used to volunteer a lot more when the kids were little, usually through the school, before we got so busy. It felt good to be back in the community again in that capacity. I didn't know I missed it." She grabbed a pair of pajamas from one of the pull-out drawers in the closet. "It was different this time with the kids being involved."

"I liked having them there," Sam said. He looked at her expression and cocked half a smile. "Don't look so surprised. I *do* like our children."

"Well, you led us very well," she said, letting the comment slide. "I think you picked the right jobs for the right people. Though poor Kyle got stuck behind that table."

"He was going to be stuck wherever he was," Sam said. "He's the only one who got to sit. I don't feel bad."

Nicole put on her pajamas and crawled under the blankets, her body sinking into the mattress. She sighed and grabbed her book from the nightstand. Who cared if it was 8:15? Sleep sounded amazing. She doubted she'd get more than a couple pages in before she was out cold.

Sam slid into bed beside her and turned on the TV. "You good if I watch while you read?"

"That's fine." The paperback was heavy in her hands as she flipped open to where she'd left off. *Definitely not more than a few pages.*

"How can you read that before bed?" Sam craned his neck and looked at the cover of the book. An abandoned, dilapidated mansion graced the cover in black and white, the title curling across the top in fanciful script: *The Vanishings of Moreland Plantation.* "Just the cover gives me the creeps."

"It's fiction. It doesn't scare me." She nestled the book onto her pillow and paused. "Sam?"

"Yeah."

"Thanks for today." The fact that he was sticking with their so-called class meant more than he could possibly know. "I really loved being together all day."

Sam flipped through three more channels, his expression pensive. His voice was so low that Nicole almost didn't hear his reply.

"Me too."

LESSON 2:

Target/Trajectory - Clarify the vision and values of your Christian family to help ensure you are all walking together on your family journey.

CHAPTER 7

Nicole clicked the seatbelt at her hip and settled back in the passenger seat. She closed her eyes and took a deep breath. She was exhausted. The last week-and-a-half had been chock-full of final dance recitals, the school Christmas program, a sock exchange, Kyle's physical therapy, and getting gifts prepared for every teacher, coach, and instructor that she could think of. She'd baked four Christmas cakes and delivered them to the neighbors, then six different cookie varieties, all of which had been carefully placed in large plastic bags and layered in tins in her freezer. To top it all off, Tyler had moved himself home for the holidays with an appalling amount of dirty laundry, and Sam had taken off for his annual golfing trip in Florida. He'd arrived home the night before last looking more relaxed than she'd seen him in ages, but she was still annoyed that he'd missed the school Christmas program for yet another year.

And she still hadn't wrapped a single present.

Sam opened the driver's side door and folded his long legs into the SUV. Tyler and Hannah were already in the backseat, Kyle's usual place now occupied by his sister as he needed easy access out of the vehicle with his crutches. Kyle sat behind Nicole, his cast-covered leg propped up on the middle seat.

Abby opened the door from the house into the garage and came running toward the vehicle, pink tablet in hand.

Sam stuck his head out the window. "No tablet, Abs. We're not going far."

"Aww, man!"

"Go get *The Candy Shop War*."

"Oh! Right!"

Nicole was thankful. Sam had started monitoring Abby's tablet time and noticed that too often it was her go-to choice for entertainment. On his own, he'd taken her out to the local bookstore and bought her a new series of books to encourage the habit of reaching for literature instead. It wasn't a hard sell as she loved to read, and Abby had been delighted. So had Nicole.

Sam tapped his fingers on the steering wheel. "I won't lie, I'm really looking forward to having more time off the next few weeks. Is this the last thing we have on the schedule before Christmas?"

Work was usually much slower during the week of Christmas after a frantic scuttle when the temperatures dropped. In years past, Sam had been antsy during his time off. This year, he had mentioned looking forward to working on the basement during his downtime more than once.

"Yes, this is it." *Thank God.* "Do you think you'll get more done on the family room this week?"

"That's the goal. I'm hoping Tyler can give me a hand too."

"What about Kyle?"

"Are you planning to carry him downstairs?"

Right. Maneuvering the basement staircase on crutches was a very bad idea. Nicole watched as Abby reappeared in the doorway, skipping to the car with a thick book clutched in her hand. "Did you grab the homework?"

Sam jabbed his thumb toward the back of the SUV as Abby climbed into the seat behind her dad. "Kyle's holding it." He waited until Abby had buckled herself into her seat before backing out of the driveway.

"I think this might have been my favorite assignment so far." Sitting down with the kids and coming up with a family vision and list of values had given Nicole a deeper glimpse into her three younger children's hearts.

Tyler had been unable to participate as he'd been back at school when they had their family meeting, but Nicole had been surprised at the depth of conversation around their table. She wasn't sure if that would have been the case a couple of months ago, but after spending the last six weeks at Grace Fellowship and hearing what Kyle and Hannah were learning at their youth group, she'd been pleased to see growth in both of them in a short amount of time. All three kids had been hesitant at first, but soon were offering up suggestions for their family values, and they all gave input as they tweaked their vision statement. The night had blessed her in more ways than one, and she and Sam had both been touched that their kids wanted their family to be more centered on Christ and relationally connected.

Now the hard part. Actually doing it.

"I hope we did it right."

Sam's comment broke Nicole out of her reverie, and she let out a small laugh. "I don't think they're grading it. They said it needs to work for us and us alone." She paused as he braked at a stop sign. "Jessica told me it's a process, so it's okay if it takes some time or we have to change something."

They sat in silence for a few minutes as Sam drove through town. Trees and houses flashed by the windows, the winter sky a dull white instead of the brilliant blue of the day before. At least it wasn't raining.

Sam frowned as he turned onto Meridian Drive and scanned the businesses lining one side of the street. "So, this thing we're going to. It's like a parenting club?"

"No, it's more of a get-together. Nothing official." Nicole pointed out the window. "I think it's on the other side of that corner store and down the side street."

Sam followed her direction and slowed the car as they approached their destination. "But it's a get-together about parenting?"

"Sort of? I think Jessica said they call it a 'Parenting Discussion' or something like that."

She spotted the building she was looking for: an old red brick and white edifice tucked back from the main road. It had been the town library for several decades before a newer and larger one had been built as the city had grown. Too historical to demolish and too old for much use, it had stood vacant and stoic for at least ten years after a short stint as a museum of local history. Then last year, a local family had rented it from the city and turned it into a bookstore and coffee shop combination.

Sam pulled the car into the last parking spot in the front of the shop. "Somehow I doubt I'm going to enjoy this as much as the community dinner. Maybe I'll pretend to be mute." Nicole rolled her eyes, and he smirked at her, his eyes taking in the hundred-year-old building. "I thought this place was empty."

"Not anymore."

"Hey, cool!" Hannah's voice piped up from the backseat. She peered out the window. "I've always wondered what it looks like in there."

The six of them piled out of the car, Kyle leading the way on his crutches. Several stone steps led to the entrance, the sides of them flanked by curling cement handrails that were wide enough to walk on. Large windows peered down at them, peeling paint visible from their place on the sidewalk and four large pillars—two on each side of the doorway— reached up to the top floor, a white stone balcony stretched between them.

Nicole loved it.

"Who needs a widow's walk? The ocean is like, a thousand miles from here." Kyle raised his eyebrows.

"I like it," Abby said, her eyes sparkling. "Can I go exploring?"

"They probably have certain places blocked off," Nicole said. "But you can look around once we get settled, okay?"

Kyle hobbled forward on his crutches and grimaced. "No wheelchair access in 1920, I guess."

Tyler gave a wicked grin. "I can give you a piggyback ride."

"I would sooner fall down these stairs and break my other leg."

Hannah and Tyler laughed and followed Kyle slowly, walking behind him to make sure he didn't fall. Sam reached out and squeezed Nicole's hand.

Abby ran up the stairs in front of them, and they brought up the rear, the glass door closing behind them with a small shudder. A tinkle of bells announced their entrance, and Nicole found herself squashed on a landing of sorts, the other five members of her family glancing around curiously.

The building was a split-level, she realized. Half a flight of stairs ran up to a gleaming, old-fashioned wooden counter with a large board menu behind it, while another half descended into the basement. Unsure of where to find their friends, Nicole opted for the top floor. At least they offered coffee.

As they neared the top of the stairs, Nicole saw that the room was much larger than she had expected. Row upon row of books stretched in aisles to the right of the coffee counter, while various tables and chairs were scattered to its left. The furniture was all mismatched and vintage, but clean. Couples were tucked into alcoves, college students were spread across tables with laptops and pages of notes, and here and there a patron was thumbing through a new book. Against the back wall leaned a shelf of neatly organized board games. Nicole smiled. She could see herself getting lost in here for hours.

"Mom, the Millers are over there." Hannah pointed to a row of books as Tom and Jessica ducked out from behind them and waved. She frowned. "Where are their kids?"

"Hey, y'all!" Tom clapped Kyle on the shoulder as they approached, his eyes taking in the crutches. "Ahhhh, yeah sorry. We didn't think through the accessibility for you, bud."

"You can buy me a donut to say you're sorry," Kyle said.

Tom laughed, his hand clutching the newest John Grisham novel. "I have to buy this anyway so you're on."

"Are Whitney and Will here?" Hannah asked.

"They're downstairs," Jessica said. "All the children's and young adult books are on the lower level next to the conference room. We told them we'd send you down when you arrived." She glanced at Kyle. "Sorry."

"No worries, I'll just hang out here with Tyler." Kyle began making his way to a vacant table as Hannah and Abby scurried downstairs to find Whitney and Will. "I'll eat my donut in front of him."

Tom gestured to the counter and the short line that had formed in front of it. "Want to get drinks first?"

"Sure," Sam said, joining him in line and perusing the menu while Nicole checked to see what Tyler and Kyle wanted to drink. "Where's Wyatt?"

"Finishing up at work. He should be here pretty soon."

"Nice." He turned to his wife as she came up to him in line. "You know what you want?"

Nicole nodded. She turned to Jessica and smiled. "I love what they've done with this building. It's so pretty." Green garland hung tastefully from the ends of shelves and draped gracefully from the edge of the counter. A Christmas tree stood in a far corner covered in red and golden baubles, and each table held a small, iron lantern with a battery-operated tea light glowing from its depths. Little springs of real greenery were tucked around them on a square of red fabric. Elegant and festive.

"They've really done an amazing job," Jessica said. "I think they've done well this year too. They've gotten popular pretty quickly." She stepped forward and ordered a caramel macchiato. "How did your family meeting go? Were you happy with it?"

"I was, actually." Nicole unwound her scarf from her neck and let it fall around her shoulders. "It was good for us to sit down together and discuss our family priorities. I thought it would be really awkward and truth be told, the kids did a fair amount of laughing at the beginning. But it didn't take long before they got into it." She smiled. "I did let Abby draw as we chatted, like you suggested. It totally worked. She didn't get bored and was able to follow along and give us some good input."

Jessica grinned. "I got that tip from another mom years ago, and I can't tell you how many times it came in handy when my kids were smaller." She stepped off to the side with Tom as Sam and Nicole gave their orders.

Tom walked over to Kyle to deliver his donut as they waited for their drinks, and Jessica turned her attention to Sam. "How about you, Sam? Did you feel like your family meeting went well?"

Sam shrugged nonchalantly. "I guess? I don't feel like I've gotten to see much of it in action since I went out of town a few days after the meeting." He looked at his wife. "Nicole said that today we're joining some sort of parenting talk?"

"Well, they call it a Parenting Discussion, but it's more of a casual hang-out time of encouragement and fellowship." The barista called Jessica's name, and she stepped over to the counter to grab hers and Tom's drinks. "Three years ago, our church partnered with another church in town with this parenting class. They did a session, and we did a session, and then we also scheduled some family-centered activities together and finished the whole thing with a little weekend conference. It was well-received, and many of the couples that did it wanted to keep in touch and

encourage each other, so they get together every quarter and catch up."
She took a sip of her macchiato. "It's been a good place to bounce parenting ideas and strategies off each other and pray together, share successes and struggles. Plus, all the kids congregate downstairs and get to reconnect. Tom and I usually try to come because we were one of the mentor couples that helped lead discussion groups at our church."

"Do you always meet here?"

"Since they opened, yes. There's good space available and plenty for the kids to do. Plus, they stock several good books on parenting here that we've recommended to a lot of couples." The barista lined drinks up on the counter. "I think you're up."

Nicole waited until all four drinks were sitting on the counter before nudging Sam. She grabbed two cups and winced. The heat from the coffee permeated the thin paper, too hot for comfort. She grabbed a handful of cardboard sleeves before making her way to where Tyler and Kyle sat playing cards at a nearby table. She set both cups in front of them. "They're super hot. I brought sleeves."

"Thanks, Mom."

"What are you playing?"

"Golf."

A family favorite. "Wyatt should be here soon. Could you check on the girls for me in about fifteen minutes?"

"Sure thing."

Nicole took her cup from Sam with a grateful smile, slipping a sleeve under the bottom of her own beverage and letting the heat warm her hands at a more comfortable temperature. She sipped carefully. The spiced chai danced on her tongue, a sweetness of vanilla at the end. She smiled. Hot drinks and books. An excellent combination.

Tom and Jessica had wandered to a table directly next to a section marked "Christian Living," and beckoned them closer. Nicole made her way over with Sam, who was already a third of the way through his Americano. The man had a mouth of steel. She pulled out one of the chairs and sat, hanging her purse on the back. "Is today just about meeting other parents who have gone through the class?" Not that she didn't like the idea. But Christmas was less than a week away, and Nicole was feeling the pressure of her mental to-do list.

"That's part of it. The other part was to show you some resources that have been helpful to us and other families who have gone through it." Tom took a long swig from his cup. "We want to be clear though. There are a lot of good books out there, and you won't connect with all of them. We want to help you guys find some resources that you think will help your particular family and situation." He wrapped his hands around his cup. "I know it's easy to assume that if a book says to do something specific, that must be the 'right way' to do it. But often, there isn't a right or wrong answer to a specific situation. It's much more about finding the right fit and doing what works for you." He swiveled his attention to Sam. "I'm sure you've experienced that in your job. You've been an electrician for what, twenty years?"

Sam took another gulp of his coffee. "Yeah, twenty-two, I think."

"Have you worked for the same company the entire time?"

Sam shook his head. "No, I've moved around. I was with one company for three years, another for six. The place I'm at now I've been with for thirteen."

Tom nodded. "Did all three companies approach jobs the same way?"

Sam shrugged. "In some ways. I mean, you have the same laws and regulations to follow no matter who you work for. But the place I first worked was largely focused on commercial property and construction."

He glanced at Nicole. "It was a good place to learn but I realized I wanted to go more into the residential side of things after Tyler was born."

"So would it be fair to say that while both commercial and residential electrician jobs are useful, there was one that you preferred and fit your life situation in a better way?"

"Oh, absolutely. One of the big reasons I went for residential was because I didn't have to travel more than forty minutes away. When I was with the first company, I could be headed anywhere in the state." Sam paused. "So you're saying that we should be looking at these parenting strategies and books in a similar way? Lots of good options, but we need to find what works for us?"

Tom grinned. "Exactly. Obviously, a lot of these books are going to have some things in common. Just like the regulations you mentioned, there are certain things that should be a part of your parenting life no matter what, like discipling your kids intentionally and making sure you're keeping open communication with them. But how you put that into action is going to vary, even from kid to kid." He slid an arm around his wife. "So, it's good to be flexible."

"We've also enjoyed revisiting some of the books we initially didn't click with," Jessica said, hands cupped around her drink. "As our kids grew and changed, we ended up seeing that our strategies had to as well."

This intrigued Nicole. She took a sip of her chai and leaned forward with interest. "Can you give us an example?"

"Sure." Jessica thought for a moment and then continued. "I suppose it would be accurate to say that we chose to put our kids in Heritage largely because we both went to private school and had a good experience. It's just what we knew." She tilted her head and rested her chin in her palm. "But when we started going through this class, I realized that I really liked the idea of homeschooling and the freedom and closeness it could give our family. I was torn. We prayed about it, and the kids were doing well in school, so we kept them at Heritage." She paused. "It was a much more intentional decision than when we had first put them in school though."

"What changed your mind?"

"Nothing bad. We both started noticing how different our life could be if we weren't tied to a school schedule. So we talked about it and prayed some more, and then decided to try home education for a year. We had some bumps along the way, but it didn't take long before we knew it had been the right call."

Nicole wrinkled her nose. "Gosh, I don't know. I've never felt the pull. I'll be honest."

Jessica's eyes twinkled as she looked across the table at them. "Remember, this is *us*. Not you. If Heritage is working well for your family, and you're happy with how your kids are growing, you may not feel that changing their educational plan is the best idea. It's good to think about though, because we found that some of our parenting decisions were based more on our own experiences than being thoughtfully intentional." She offered an encouraging smile. "Even if you keep things the same after thinking through things, you can gain a renewed sense of why you've chosen what you have."

Nicole paused. "We actually need to do that with dance." She turned to Sam. "I have to sign the girls up for next semester and brought the forms home with me yesterday, but maybe we should talk about things before we make that commitment. It's gotten pretty demanding."

Sam smirked. "Fine by me. But if you pull Hannah from dance, I'm not the one who's going to tell her. She'll kill the messenger."

Nicole grimaced. "It's true. But the dance schedule is getting ridiculous. I mean, she's twelve." She looked at Tom and Jessica. "She did a theater class this semester that she really enjoyed, but she couldn't do the school play because it conflicted with dance." She shrugged. "I don't know, I'm afraid dance is hyper-focusing Hannah on one hobby to the exclusion of others, and I'd like her to be able to explore some of her other interests." She looked at Sam. "Do we think she's going to dance professionally? Would we even want her to live that kind of life?"

Sam raised his eyebrows. "Well, you've apparently been thinking about this much more than I have."

Nicole took another sip of her drink. "She has a lot of talents. It would be good if she had more chances to explore them."

"What about Kyle?" Jessica asked. "Obviously he's done sports like his brother, but he said he's out the remainder of the year because of his leg."

"Sports isn't Kyle's passion, but he likes them fine," Nicole said. "They give him something to do with his friends. Tyler's always loved the game, but for Kyle's it's been more about the camaraderie of being a team."

Tom tapped the lid of his now-empty cup. "What's he into aside from sports?"

Sam looked at Nicole, a slightly ashamed look on his face. "Nic?"

"His friends. He likes to read and play his Xbox." Nicole thought for a moment. "He's always liked computers. A lot of the books I've seen him with lately have to do with coding. He's taking a robotics class next semester too, now that I think of it. He had mentioned doing it last year, but they do their big tournaments in the late winter. He had to pass because of basketball." She smiled. "Silver lining of a broken leg: robots don't care if you're on crutches."

Sam sat back in his chair. "He didn't tell me that." He glanced over at his sons. Wyatt had joined them at some point during their conversation, and the three of them had spread a board game over their table. "That's really cool."

Motion caught the corner of Nicole's eye, and she turned her head to see Hannah and Abby hurrying over from downstairs. A beaming smile lit Abby's face. "Mom! I won three rounds of Go Fish in a row!"

"Really? Nice job!" Nicole reached behind her daughter's head and adjusted the scrunchie holding her hair back in a ponytail. "Did you have fun?"

"Yep!"

"Where's Whit and Will?" Tom asked. The younger two Miller kids hadn't followed them.

Hannah motioned to the staircase. "Setting up a new game."

Abby bounced on her tiptoes. "They said they'd teach us to play one called Five Crowns."

"Oh, that's fun," Jessica said. "We play that one a lot."

"Can we get something to drink too?" Hannah gestured to Nicole's almost-empty cup.

"Sure." Nicole fished in her purse for her wallet and pulled out a ten-dollar bill. "No coffee."

"I *know*." Hannah made a face and took the money. "Can we get peppermint hot chocolate?"

"Go for it."

Abby squealed and clapped her hands together, dashing off after Hannah as the two of them made their way to the coffee counter.

"It's sweet that they picked a game that Abby could play," Nicole said, draining the last of her chai and setting the cup back on the table.

"It's nice that they're getting *along*," Sam said, his eyes following his daughters.

Tom laughed. "Siblings. Never a dull moment." He glanced at his watch. "We have a couple minutes before people will start to arrive, so I can wrap this up. The title of this session is 'Explore Your Options,' and basically they just want to emphasize what we already have: There are no perfect parents, no two families are exactly alike, and you want to make informed and intentional decisions that reflect your family vision and values." He pointed to the bookshelf behind them. "Have either of you read many books on parenting?"

Sam let out a bark of a laugh. "No."

Nicole shook her head. "I read one or two when Tyler was a baby, but once Kyle came along I stopped. I might still have a couple at home."

"Oh, it's so hard to find time to read when you have tiny kids," Jessica said. "I remember feeling like reading was too much effort when I was so tired. I just wanted TV."

"She falls asleep as soon as the TV goes on," Sam said.

Tom and Jessica laughed. "When we went through this class, our instructor encouraged us to read solid parenting books from a biblical perspective together. He gave us a list of several good ones that he recommended. They stock some of them here."

Nicole raised her eyebrows at Jessica. "How'd you get Tom to agree to read a book with you?"

Tom held up his hands. "I don't mind reading, but I really prefer audiobooks. Plus, my commute was about twenty-five minutes at the time." He shrugged. "She got a paper copy, and I bought it on Audible. It was a lot more enjoyable for me to listen to the book than sit down and read it."

Jessica grinned. "He actually finished it before me, even though I stuck my copy in my purse and read it at dentist appointments and sports practices."

Nicole looked at Sam. "That could work. You listen to podcasts in your truck all the time. You could just pretend the book is a really long one."

Sam cocked his head. "I can give it a try."

Tom stood up from the table. "If you guys like podcasts, we can recommend some good ones. There's one for dads that I really like."

"Yeah, I usually listen to mine when I'm working around the house," said Jessica. "I used to put on music, but I like the podcasts better. They make cleaning the bathrooms go faster."

Nicole and Sam followed Tom and Jessica over to the shelves of Christian Living books. The parenting section was bigger than she expected. "Are any of your favorites here?"

Tom perused the shelf for a moment, pulling out a book here and there until he had a stack of four in his hands. "Feel free to look at whatever you'd like, but I'd start with one of these. They're all about raising kids in the middle years—you know, past toddlerhood and preschool." He tapped one of the covers. "You guys pick one, and we'll buy it for you. Consider it a Christmas present." He glanced over Nicole's shoulder and waved at someone across the room. "People are starting to arrive so let Jessica know what you decide before we leave, and we'll be happy to grab it for you." He handed Nicole the stack of books and his eyes twinkled as he looked at Sam. "Don't look so worried. I'll buy you an Audible credit."

* * *

"So what did you think?"

Nicole was tugging her arms into her coat when Jessica appeared at her side, the chosen book wrapped tightly in brown parcel paper and stuck in a red bag. "I actually had a great time." It was true. The conversations she'd been able to have with people she'd barely met had shocked her. Her struggles and worries, her hopes and desires for her family, so many of the women she'd spoken with had similar stories. She had thought she was alone for a long time. Apparently, she was entirely average.

"Oh, good!" Jessica handed over the bag. "I hope it was encouraging."

"It really was." Nicole zipped up her coat and wound her scarf around her neck. "I feel like I learned a lot just by listening to a bunch of their experiences." She held up her phone. "I'm going out to coffee with Audrey after Christmas. We kind of hit it off. At least, I think we did."

"Audrey Jamison? Oh, she's great." Jessica smiled at Sam as he came up beside Nicole. "How'd it go, Sam?"

"Good. I actually knew one of the guys and his wife. They've been clients of mine for about five years." Sam chuckled. "He was shocked to see me, but we had a good time catching up."

Nicole stuck her hands in her pockets, the bag trapped on her forearm. "It was helpful to see that being intentional and keeping at this can make a difference. Hearing that other people have had similar struggles and have worked through them is motivating."

Jessica gave Nicole a hug as Tom shook Sam's hand. "It will be a few weeks before we

meet again, so your homework can be starting the book and listening to a podcast or two on your downtime." He wrapped his arm around Jessica. "Keep it simple for the holidays."

Nicole breathed a sigh of relief. She wasn't sure she could handle anything more before Christmas.

Snow was falling in a light shower when the six of them left the shop, their breath clearly visible under the streetlights. Sam helped Kyle down the stairs as he maneuvered over the dusted concrete while Nicole unlocked the SUV and turned it on to heat up. She rubbed her hands together, wishing she'd thought to bring gloves, then turned in her seat to talk to Abby. "Did you win the other game?

Abby shook her head. "Will did."

"Yeah, but Whitney was ahead till the last round," Hannah said. "By the way, I want that game. Can I put it on my Christmas list?"

"Probably." Nicole needed another stocking stuffer for Hannah anyway. She looked at Tyler. "Did you and Wyatt have a good time catching up?"

Tyler was on his phone, thumbs clicking across the screen as he texted. "Yeah, it was good. He told me more about his internship." Tyler glanced up at Nicole and dropped his phone into the cupholder beside him. "Must be nice to get paid to learn."

"It's a paid internship?"

"Yeah, his work and school are kind of linked together." He drummed his fingers on his knee. "He has a Christmas volunteer thing he's doing on Tuesday and invited me to go. You don't mind, right?"

Nicole blinked. Had Tyler just semi-asked permission to do something? Something in service to other people? She worked to make her voice casual. "Of course not." Next time she saw Jessica, she needed to make sure to tell her how much she appreciated her son's influence on Tyler.

Kyle opened the door and slid into his seat. He handed his crutches to Sam, who firmly shut the door behind him. Nicole gave him an encouraging smile. "You have an okay time? Sorry you couldn't make it downstairs."

"Nah, it was fine. Wyatt told a few of the guys about my predicament, and they came up to our table." He rubbed under his arm where the crutches dug into him. "Dude, I will not miss those things."

"Meet any new friends?"

Kyle looked at her, bemused. "Sure, Mom. And they brought me a juice box."

Hannah laughed from the back seat. "Well, *I* met some new people who were really nice. And two were girls from school, but they're a year younger than me." She settled back in her chair. "Abby and I had fun together, right Abs?"

"Yes!"

The back door opened and slammed as Sam tossed Kyle's crutches into the back of the vehicle.

"Hey Mom, have you heard of a place called Endeavor?"

"Hmm? I don't think so."

Kyle was typing in the name on his phone's search engine. "I guess it's a camp that's all about tech learning. One of the guys at the coffee shop goes every summer and was telling me about it." He scrolled through the Google results. "I might not be able to do any of the sports camps for school, so I thought I might look into doing it instead."

More tech interest from Kyle. Nicole made a mental note and nodded at him. "Do some research and tell me what you find." Sam opened the driver's side door and climbed into his seat. "Your dad and I can talk about it once we get more details."

"What are we talking about?" Sam jammed his finger onto the heater's button and turned it up to the highest setting.

"Kyle wants to maybe go to a summer camp for tech. But there's no rush." Nicole crossed her legs and leaned back in her chair. "What do you think about the assignment?"

Sam shrugged. "It's fine. I'm glad it isn't a lot of work this time. I want to enjoy my vacation." He looked at Kyle in the rearview mirror. "A tech camp, huh? Could be cool."

"Yeah, maybe." Non-committal. Such a teenage boy.

Sam let the silence hang for a moment before addressing him again. "You like tech stuff, Kyle?"

Kyle looked up from his phone at his dad. "Yeah, I guess."

"I have to set up some sort of audiobook subscription to read a book with your mom. Do you think you could help me out with that?"

Kyle raised his eyebrows. "You mean like an Audible account?" He let out a snort. "You're going to read?"

Sam let the comment slide and Nicole was thankful. "Yep. Can you set me up?"

Kyle shrugged. "Sure."

"Thanks."

The corner of Sam's mouth twitched in the slightest indication of a smile, and Nicole bit her lip to keep one off her own face. She knew this wasn't Sam's idea of a fun activity, but he was truly putting forth the effort—with her, with Abby, and now with Kyle. Nicole rested her elbow on the cool lip of the window and watched snowflakes dance in a whirl of wind under the light of a lamppost.

A warm joy spread through her chest.

It was the best gift he could have given her.

LESSON 3:

Explore Options - There are many ways to parent. Take time to explore options that might be more consistent with your Christian family vision and values.

CHAPTER 8

"Why are we meeting at Home Depot?" The question came from Hannah, who was curled up in the back of the van with her nose in a book. She glanced up for a moment and raised her eyebrows. "Are we building something?"

"That'd be cool," Tyler said. "I've been meaning to go to Home Depot with Dad anyway." He whipped out his phone and began typing something into his search engine. "Basement...bar...with...cabinets...."

Nicole drove down Meridian and turned left onto Jefferson Avenue. Snow was pushed to the sides of the street, fresh from yesterday's snowplow. Most of the piles were still white with new snow, but the roads were brown and muddy with slush. Her SUV was going to need serious attention after this latest dumping.

"I want to play games again!" This came from Abby, her lower lip stuck out in a small pout.

"We played games the last two times," Hannah reminded her. "We'll probably do something else, but it will still be fun. We always have a good time with Whitney and Will."

The road curved to the right, and Nicole eased onto a new road. Home Depot was up ahead, the parking lot remarkably empty for a snowy Saturday in January.

"Is Dad there yet?" Hannah craned her neck to see out the window. Sam had taken Kyle to his physical therapy appointment, and the two of them were meeting the rest of the family when they were finished.

"I see his truck!" Abby pointed out the window, curls bouncing in excitement. "Awww, they beat us!"

Nicole turned into the Home Depot parking lot and pulled next to Sam's truck. He and Kyle were in the cab, sipping large sodas and sharing a sickeningly large basket of french fries.

Kyle rolled down his window as the rest of his family piled out of the vehicle. "'Sup, family!"

"You got fries?" Abby stood on tiptoe and reached for one. "No fair!"

Kyle dangled a couple just out of her reach, then promptly ate them. "We got done early," he said around a mouthful of fries.

"Ewww, close your mouth!" Hannah wrinkled her nose. "You're so gross."

"Dad, can we look at some stuff for the basement while we're here?" Tyler said, his eyes darting between Hannah and Kyle. He walked to the back of the truck and grabbed Kyle's crutches out of the bed. "I had some ideas for the family room, but I'm not sure if they'll fit into our budget."

Sam's voice floated out of the window. "Sure, sounds good."

Nicole smiled to herself. Sam had had the excellent idea to make the most of Tyler's time home over Christmas break. The two of them were working on the basement together almost every evening—Sam had been making a point to be home by dinner—and it had quickly morphed into a father-son project. Granted, part of the purpose was for Tyler to pay back his parents for helping pay his Minor in Possession ticket, but the two of them seemed to be enjoying the time together as well. Nicole had been surprised at how interested Tyler was in learning about home construction. Growing up, he and Sam had always bonded over sports, but it looked as though they had even more in common than she had originally thought.

Kyle opened the passenger side door and grabbed his crutches from Tyler. "Thanks, man." He hooked his arms over the pads. "Think they still have Christmas lights? I want to stock up for next year while they're cheap. I had three strands burn out on me this year."

"What do you mean, 'you'? You stayed on the ground and yelled up at Dad and Tyler this year," Nicole said.

Kyle looked at her in mock offense. "Excuse me. It's hard work telling everyone how to bring life to my Christmas light displays."

Nicole heard the other door slam, and a moment later, Sam came around the back of the truck, a tube of blueprints in his hand. "Guess what I finished?" He waved his phone in the air.

Nicole looked at him blankly. "A phone call?"

"No, that book." Sam grinned. "Finished it while Kyle was doing his physical therapy."

"Really?" Nicole had finished her copy the week before and had been too afraid to ask Sam how his audio experience was going. A smile spread across her face. "That's awesome. What'd you think?"

Sam fell into step beside his wife as their kids walked ahead toward the heavy glass doors. Wind whipped across Nicole's face, and she snuggled her nose down into her scarf. Winter wasn't as fun after Christmas was over.

"I actually didn't mind listening to it. Parts I really enjoyed." Sam took her gloved hand in his. "The author talked about parenting in a way I hadn't heard of before. It was—I don't know—holistic maybe?" He kicked a piece of ice out of the way with his boot. "The chapter on fathers really made me think. I ended up listening to it twice." He watched Abby skip into the store. "I never considered how much influence a dad has on his children."

Nicole squeezed his hand. "I'm glad you liked it. Have you tried any of the podcasts?" She'd been making a habit of putting one on whenever she was cleaning or in the car.

"Not yet. I wanted to get through the book first since it was due today. Cutting it close, I guess." He winked at her and then glanced at his watch. "Do you know how long this is supposed to take? My boss texted and said he needs a phone meeting with me at twelve."

"I don't know, but if you need to leave a little early, I'm sure that's fine. Just tell them if we're getting close, and you need to cut out."

They walked the rest of the way in a comfortable silence. The glass doors slid open as they approached, and Nicole glanced around for their kids. The four of them were standing off to the left with Tom and Jessica, who were chatting them up cheerfully. The Miller kids, however, were nowhere in sight.

"We were supposed to bring the kids, right?" Sam had noticed the conspicuous absence as well.

"Oh, totally," Jessica gave a nod of agreement. "Ours were supposed to be here—"

"Whitney's sick," Abby said, her face falling in disappointment.

Nicole ran a hand over her daughter's hair. "Don't interrupt, sweet pea," she said gently. She looked at Jessica. "Everything okay?"

"Well, technically Whitney and Will are both sick, though Will's finally up and about today." Tom adjusted his baseball cap. "We started the new year with the flu."

"Oh no!" Nicole grimaced in pity. "I'm sorry. That's rough. Did you all get it?"

"Five for five," Jessica said. "Tom's brother and his family came over for New Year's Eve, and we caught it from them. They got sick on the first, and Wyatt and I came down with it a few days later."

"Then me, then Will." Tom gave a half-smile. "We thought Whit was going to skip it because she held out so long, but she crashed yesterday.

Will's on day five." He held up a hand. "I've been completely symptom-free for three days and fever free for five. Scouts honor."

"Oh, I'm not worried. It's everywhere." Nicole hitched her purse higher on her shoulder. "I'm at least glad you weren't sick over Christmas."

Jessica clapped her hands together, eyes sparkling. "Speaking of! How was your holiday? We haven't seen you guys since the Christmas Eve service!"

"Really, really good." Nicole felt a flutter of delight at the truth of the words. It had been her favorite Christmas of the past several years. The pace of life had been different. Since they hadn't traveled anywhere, she hadn't had to deal with the additional frenzy of packing or frantically checking incoming storm systems that could derail their plans. Everyone seemed happy to be home, and with all their activities canceled for two solid weeks, the amount of free time had provided all of them with a breath of fresh air. Nicole didn't think it was a coincidence that with everyone being more intentional in spending time together, Christmas had gone so smoothly.

"Sam had almost the whole week of Christmas off, which was amazing," Nicole said, beaming. "He and Tyler have spent a lot of time working on the basement together, and it's been fun to see it coming along."

"It's been interesting, actually," Tyler said, shoving his hands in his pockets. "Dad taught me how to do some simple wiring, and I was surprised how much I liked it. He let me do one section of the family room by myself."

Kyle gave a solemn nod. "So, when our house goes up in flames, we know why."

Tom laughed. "Careful. If he follows in your dad's footsteps, he might not give you a family discount if you razz him too much."

Sam gave a half-smile. "I did check the work. We should be fireproof." He looked at Tyler, and Nicole could see the pride in his eyes. "Tyler did great. We've had a good time together in the basement." Sam turned to Kyle. "As soon as you can stand on two feet, I'm dragging you down there too."

"Hard pass." Kyle rolled his eyes. But Nicole saw the grin lurking at the edges of his mouth.

"We played a lot of Five Crowns," Hannah said. "I got it in my stocking."

"Five Crowns and Ticket to Ride and Settlers of Catan..." Kyle ticked games off on his fingers.

"Sounds like you guys had a lot of good family time," Jessica said, giving Nicole a knowing eyebrow raise.

"We did." Nicole gave a contented sigh. "Both Sam and I felt like we got a glimpse of how life could be if we continue on this path. It was encouraging."

"Um, hello? Is no one going to mention my amazing light display?" Kyle rocked back and forth on his crutches. "It was my best one yet."

"Ahhh, yes. Kyle designs a new display each year and puts it up with Sam." Nicole bit back a laugh. "This year he had to direct from the driveway. It was...interesting."

"He was a drama queen," Hannah said.

"Not true," Kyle said. "You all lacked vision."

Tyler shook his head. "Own the drama, Kyle. You were a diva."

Tom threw back his head and laughed. "Remind me to drive by your house next year. I want to see this."

Sam held up the blueprints he was holding. "I am curious what you're planning to have us do with these." He spun them absentmindedly in his hands. "Oh, and we both finished the homework."

"The book was great," Nicole said.

"Excellent." Tom took the blueprints from Sam and beckoned them away from the store entrance. "I wanted you to bring these because I know it's been an ongoing project, and Jess and I were interested in what you're planning to do." He turned down an aisle and led them into the kitchen section. "There's a lot of counters here. Can we spread them out?"

Sam gently unrolled the blueprints over an oversized island, his hands flattening out the corners. One side wouldn't stay down, so he dropped his keys onto it as a makeshift paperweight.

Tom's eyes glanced over the paper. "Richardson kids, I want to hear from you. What are you most excited about in the basement?"

Hannah's hand shot into the air. "Definitely the family room. We're going to finally get a big TV and put it down there so we can watch movies, and we're going to get a ping-pong table too." She looked at her brothers. "I wanted air hockey but was outvoted. But ping pong will still be really fun!"

Tyler shrugged. "Well, I live at college most of the time, so I don't know how excited I am about it, but I have to say my favorite part is the man cave because it's where Dad and I watch football."

Tom pointed at Abby. "How about you, Abby?"

Abby grinned. "Daddy said he'd build me a special place to read. Kind of like a window seat but without a window."

"I always wanted a window seat when I was a kid," Jessica said. She nodded to Kyle. "How about you?"

Kyle cocked his head. "I'd probably say the family room because with a big TV, having friends over to play video games will be a lot of fun." He looked at his dad. "But the man cave is cool too."

"Yeah, I'd pick the man cave too," Sam said. "If adults get to vote."

Nicole felt a stab of annoyance that Sam had picked his man cave over their family room. She swallowed, fighting against the temptation to take his comment personally. "I'd say the family room. Our living room upstairs is nice but isn't very big. It can feel a little crowded if all six of us are in it or if company is over." She forced a smile. "The family room will be big with lots of space to spread out. Watching movies and playing games will be really comfortable down there." She paused for a moment. "I like the little craft room too, but I haven't spent as much time down there lately."

Tom gave an encouraging nod. "All of you are excited about the basement getting finished, that's obvious. It's a vision you all share, and I think everyone sees the benefit of working to get it done." He pointed at Sam and Tyler. "Obviously you two are doing the heavy lifting right now, but will everyone be contributing to the painting and decorating?"

"Oh, for sure." Nicole couldn't wait until they reached that stage of the process. "We haven't made any of those decisions yet though."

Tom tapped the blueprints. "Your vision for the basement is a lot like your vision for your family. Everyone is on board and pointed at a common, overarching goal."

"And that goal is going to help determine details that you haven't even thought about yet," Jessica said. "You know the floor plans of your basement remodel, but what color will you be painting everything? What photos will hang on the walls? Are you going to replace any of the flooring and if so, with what?"

Nicole looked at Sam. "We haven't gotten that far yet."

"Which is totally fine," Tom said. "There is a natural order to this. You have to finish remodeling before painting the walls. You have to finish painting before hanging photos." He began rolling up the blueprints. "Similarly, your family vision can help you determine how to handle life details."

Nicole frowned. "I'm understanding you in theory, but once again, I need an example."

"It's easy to compartmentalize our lives if we aren't being intentional," Jessica said. "A family can have a great vision statement that they're all excited about without taking into consideration how it affects things in their lives other than those things that are obviously spiritual." She tucked her hands into her coat pockets. "Things like how you discipline your kids, what education you give them, how you handle medical decisions, or which activities you enroll your family in. These aren't things we usually consider to be related to our faith at first glance, but they will affect the spiritual lives of our families. Your family vision should directly affect how you process and make decisions about those life specifics, just like your vision for the basement will help guide you in putting it together."

Sam nodded in understanding. "So, an example could be not enrolling a child in a good activity if it would take away too much family time and cause relationship problems."

"Great example," Tom said. "We're going to come back to this in a bit, but first I want to focus on your basement." He tapped his open palm with the tube. "I remember you mentioning that there were a few cosmetic changes you wanted to make to the already-finished side." He looked at Nicole. "Is that right?"

"Yeah, the finished side is mostly fine, but there are a few tweaks we wanted to make."

"Such as?"

Nicole thought for a moment. "We need new hardware in the bathroom because there's a lot of hard water build up on the shower head and the faucet squeaks no matter what we do to it. And then I wanted to take out the carpet in the craft room and replace it with linoleum so that I don't have to worry about paint ruining it." She paused. "I also wanted to paint the spare room."

"Perfect." Tom handed the blueprints to Sam and rested his hands on his hips. "That's your assignment for today: picking out hardware for the bathroom, choosing flooring for the craft room, and picking out a paint color for the extra bedroom. We clear?"

A small thrill ran down Nicole's spine. Things were starting to come together. "Crystal."

***

"How did it go?"

Jessica's encouraging smile met them as the Richardsons gathered back at the kitchen section to meet the Millers. Nicole and Hannah held up three small jars of paint. "I wanted to try a couple colors before coming back and picking one out. Sometimes they look better on the strip."

Sam grimaced comically. "They all look exactly the same. They're blue."

"One has green undertones, and one is slightly lighter than the other two."

"You're making that up."

Tom chuckled and motioned to Tyler. "Find a good option for the bathroom?"

"Yeah, I think so." Tyler studied the faucet in his hand. "The old one was brass but didn't really match since the shower hardware is chrome and the vanity handles are brushed nickel. I liked the nickel best and Dad agreed, so we got that one."

"We helped Mom pick out the floor," Abby said. "It's white and grey and looks kind of like tile."

"Very nice," Jessica said. "Was it hard to choose?"

"Not for the bathroom. The paint was probably hardest." Sam looked at Nicole and she nodded in agreement. "There were so many color options, I thought I'd go cross-eyed. I don't know why, but I always assumed we'd paint that room green."

"And I'd assumed yellow because I wanted something bright and cheery," Nicole said.

Sam cracked a smile. "And I hate yellow."

"Well, you had a good point. Yellow in a basement can look garish." Nicole held out her paint swatches. "So, we compromised. Light blue keeps things bright enough to be cheerful but is much less likely to cause issues with the lighting." She grinned at Sam. "Plus, he likes blue."

"This is true."

Tom leaned his hip onto one of the counters. "You guys are going to be confronted with a lot of choices in parenting." He nodded at the swatches. "A lot of options, if you will. Jess touched on some of them: education, medical stuff, discipline, etc. There are tons of other ones too: How you use technology, the way your family communicates, what you do for dinner, certain demands of your job. The list goes on." Tom crossed his arms. "There are a lot of ways to handle each of these things. Some choices will be costly but have a great future return." He nodded to the kids. "Tuition at Heritage isn't cheap, but your desire is for your children to have a grounded, biblical education. You're playing the long game. And not just for your own kids. These choices will affect the way they choose to parent your future grandchildren."

"You're saying to do the hard thing, rather than the easy thing because of the payoff," Sam said.

"Yes, for the most part. Or sometimes compromise is necessary and good. Just make sure you're compromising on the details and not your family vision itself."

"It helps to write things down," Jessica said, "which also happens to be one of the lessons of this session."

Sam raised his eyebrows. "Writing stuff down is the lesson?"

"It's about starting the habit and keeping things straight," Tom said. "There are a lot of details to discuss with parenting, and tons of ways to get distracted from your family vision. Writing things down makes sure everyone is on the same page and nothing gets forgotten."

"That's basically your homework," Jessica said with a grin. "Going over those categories that are most important to your family right now and writing out your plan for each." She handed Nicole a small pamphlet. "This has several questions to help guide your discussion, if you need some inspiration."

Nicole took the pamphlet and smiled. "Thanks. This will be much appreciated, I'm sure." She looked at Sam. "You good with this plan?"

"Yep." Sam glanced at his watch and then reached for his wallet. "But I also have a phone call with my boss in half an hour so we should probably check out and head home."

***

"Nic? You have a sec?"

Sam poked his head into the kitchen and beckoned her into the living room. Nicole was spreading mayonnaise on several slices of bread, deli bags of turkey and roast beef lined up at attention. "Sure." She motioned to Hannah, who was slicing apples. "When you're done, can you start working on the sandwiches? Three turkey, three beef."

"Does everyone want tomato and lettuce?"

"Everyone except Abby."

"Okay."

Nicole stepped out of the kitchen and followed Sam into the living room. "Everything okay?" He didn't seem upset, but he obviously had something he wanted to discuss.

"I just got off with Jeff." Sam ran a hand through his hair and looked at her. He seemed...excited? Maybe. But if he was, it was laced with a large dose of hesitancy.

Nicole folded her arms. "Did something go wrong on a job?"

"No, not at all." Sam mirrored her, folding his arms across his chest. He planted both feet in a ready stance on the floor and studied her. "One of our supervisors is leaving the company."

That could be good or bad. "Which one? Did something happen?"

Sam shook his head. "It's Dave. Nothing bad. He just got a great offer in Sumerlin, and he couldn't pass it up." He paused. "But that means his position will be opening up. Jeff wants me to apply for the job. He asked if he could mention me to the hiring committee because they usually take his recommendation seriously."

Nicole bit her lip. *Supervisor?* She didn't know much about the positions above Sam, but she knew enough to know that this was a big deal. And a big commitment. "Do you know how much would change for you if you took it?"

"A hefty pay raise, for one." Sam rubbed his chin. "That alone makes it very appealing." He cocked his head. "But it also means more hours and more responsibility. I'd have to travel more than I do now because I'd be over an entire state region, not just the Devon Falls area."

Panic and sadness curled inside of Nicole's belly. "What did you tell him?"

Sam watched her face. "I told him he was free to mention me, but that I'd need to talk to you before I decided to apply." A cloud passed over his face. "I know this is a big ask. But it also has some incredible potential."

Nicole rubbed her arms. It was an amazing opportunity for Sam's career. They both knew it. *But what about us?* What about the progress they were finally making? Sam was connecting with their kids in ways he hadn't in years. They were spending more time together as a couple. Their family was building deeper relationships. It could all be gone in a flash if he took a job that placed Sam right back into his old patterns of long work hours and relational absence. But could she ask him not to do it when he was the one who bore the burden of providing for their family?

Nicole took a deep breath and rubbed the back of her neck. "I don't know, Sam." She locked eyes with him, willing him to understand. "I'm not saying that you shouldn't do it, but I do have some real concerns." She forced calm into her voice. "I think we should pray about it. Together. And do that homework from today. It might help us figure out how we feel about it."

Sam nodded. "I can live with that. In fact, I think that's a good idea." He picked up his phone from the side table and opened the messaging tab. "Are you okay with me telling him I'll let him know in the next week?"

"A week sounds good." Nicole blinked away tears, the possibility of losing everything they'd worked for in the past couple of months flashing before her mind's eye. "Maybe ask him specifics about the time commitment?"

Sam's fingers flew across his phone. "And...done." He pocketed it and walked over to her, wrapping his arms around her. He rested his chin on top of her head. "Thanks for being open to it."

Nicole swallowed, a hot tear spilling onto the cheek leaning against Sam's shoulder. "Thanks for checking with me first."

She hated the idea of losing him to his job again, but the fact that he had asked for her blessing before applying was a big step in a good direction.

LESSON 4:

Write it Down - Take time to put into words and write down a parenting plan that will keep your family focused on your journey.

CHAPTER 9

"**N**ic? Can you bring down some pop?"

Sam's call drifted up the basement stairs to the kitchen where Nicole was up to her elbows in dishwater. She glanced at the clock and nearly choked. "It's 9:30! Why on earth do you need pop?" The breakfast dishes weren't even done yet.

"Mom, it's basically just bubbly coffee," Kyle said. "You're not going to deny us our vital caffeine buzz, right?"

Kyle was finally off his crutches and back on his feet, much to the delight of everyone in the family. He wasn't allowed to do much more than walk—doctor's orders—but being able to maneuver stairs and sharp corners by himself was a luxury in which he was reveling. Nicole smiled to herself. He'd even started joining Tyler and Sam down in the basement as they worked, and she was certain that a lot more laughter was coming from down below now that all three Richardson men were together. The sound was sweet.

"Fine. What kind?"

"Two Cokes and a Dr. Pepper."

Nicole dried her hands on a dishtowel and made her way to the fridge. She opened it and scanned the cans lining the inside of the door. "We're out of Dr. Pepper. What do you want instead?"

"Aww, man," Kyle said. "Hannah drank it all, didn't she?"

"Considering that both girls and you drink it, I'm sure it was a group effort. What's your backup?"

"Mountain Dew."

More like battery acid. That stuff always gave Nicole a headache. "Okay, sounds good." She pulled the three sodas out of the fridge and pushed the door closed with her hip.

Lights were on all over the basement as Nicole descended the stairs, a soda in each hand and one pressed between her forearm and her ribs. Sam took them from her with his thanks and passed them around to Tyler and Kyle, who popped the tops of their cans and started chugging.

Sam grinned at her. "It's looking really good."

It was. Nicole's eyes scanned the basement in delight. The bathroom hardware had been replaced, along with the flooring in the craft room. The wiring behind the walls of the family room was finished. All that remained was the work of external outlets and cables so that they could plug in their electronics and internet. The drywall was mostly finished. Nicole was hoping they'd be done today. And then, the finishing work— texturing, painting, and installing the floor —could begin. Sam was optimistic they would be functional by spring break. After that, she could start decorating.

"I'm realizing I got the shaft at the community dinner," Kyle said, slapping a newly finished wall with the palm of his hand. "I got stuck behind that table serving drinks and didn't get to hang with Dad. Who knew he was fun?"

"You were newly broken and needed to sit," Sam said. "But don't worry. When this is done, we can attack another project."

Nicole felt her heart do a little dance. The basement project was acting as some sort of lifeline between Kyle and Sam. It was good to know that when it was done, they wanted to keep it going.

"So the boys and I were starting to talk about the summer." Sam opened his pop with a fizzing sound and took a few large gulps. "You know, where we want to go for our family vacation and what we want to do." He rested a hand on his hip. "We were thinking of maybe doing that Mexico resort again like last year."

"Really?" Nicole wasn't sure what surprised her more: the fact that Sam wanted to go back to the same place two years in a row, or the fact that she didn't feel any excitement about it. She crossed her arms and squinted in concentration. "I guess I didn't feel like that was one of our favorite vacations."

Sam nodded. "I know I was too into work when we went, but I thought maybe a do-over would be a good idea. Make some better memories."

"Maybe." She wanted to be supportive, but the draw just wasn't there. "Can we talk about it with the girls? I'd like to consider some other options."

Now it was Sam's turn to look surprised. "You have another place you want to go?"

"Not necessarily." Nicole looked at Tyler and Kyle. "Do you guys have any ideas off the top of your heads?"

"As long as it doesn't conflict with Endeavor, I don't really care when we go." Kyle downed the rest of his soda. "Mexico was cool. But I could go somewhere else too."

"Same here," Tyler said, side-eying his brother. "Except I don't care about missing some nerdy camp."

Kyle wagged his head at his brother and raised his eyebrows. "Don't diss the computer geniuses. One day, we'll be the ones that stop the robots from taking over the world."

"Yeah, robots you made in the first place."

Kyle shrugged. "Touché."

Nicole laughed and rubbed her neck. "Can I think about it?"

"Sure. Ask the girls too." Sam glanced at his watch. "Okay, boys. Break's over. If we want to be done by the time we have to meet the Millers this evening, we need to wrap up here by three so we can put stuff away and shower." He cocked his head and studied his wife. "You okay?"

"Yes, I'm fine. The basement looks amazing." Nicole gave him a reassuring smile and turned toward the stairs. "Want me to bring you down lunch at noon?"

"That'd be great, babe. Thanks."

Nicole climbed the stairs at a slow pace, her hand gently sliding up the railing as she turned the idea of Mexico over in her mind. Why didn't she want to go? She honestly wasn't sure. There was nothing wrong with taking a vacation like it. Maybe the memories of feeling so disconnected were affecting her more than she realized.

Would it be just like last time? Probably not. Nicole reached the top of the stairs and rolled up her sleeves as walked to the sink full of half-washed dishes. They were doing better. She and Sam both felt it. They'd put together their parenting plan, and while Nicole had enjoyed going over it with Sam and feeling like they were on the same page, she also felt they were at a loss over what to do with it. It was as though they'd gone and purchased a car, and then realized neither of them knew how to drive.

Nicole turned on the sink and plunged her hands into the soapy water. Tyler was doing better, and for that she was thankful. She also didn't feel like she could take much credit for it. He'd been home for the better part of a month over Christmas break but was due to head back to college after church on Sunday. Her stomach burned. She wished she had more confidence that he would make wise decisions when he was out from under their roof. He'd been hanging out quite a bit with Wyatt when he was free, but there was no Wyatt at his dorm. Nicole bit her lip. *How long will he last this time?* She felt a wave of immediate guilt as the thought flashed through her mind. What kind of loving mother had so little confidence in her son?

She shook her head to clear it. Tyler wouldn't have any games this semester, just conditioning. He seemed almost relieved about it and had mentioned more than once that the extra time would be good for his studies. Nicole sent up a silent prayer. *Forgive me, Lord. Protect him from himself and from anyone who would harm him. Give him the strength he needs to be wise.* Prayer was her best defense. She needed to remember that.

Kyle was thriving, for which she sent up another quick prayer, this time in thanks. Joining the robotics class due to his broken leg was quickly proving to be one of the best results of the whole debacle. Sam had been right: Kyle was a natural. And he *loved* all the tech involved. They'd told him he could go to Endeavor during the summer, and he had already read two books from the camp's recommended reading list. Nicole knew that he joked about being a computer genius, but she wouldn't be surprised at all if he ended up doing tech as a career. He seemed to have found his niche.

Nicole opened the dishwasher and continued her mental assessment of each of her children. Hannah and Abby were doing okay. They'd hit a high point at Christmas when they'd both been home together and dance-free. With friends being gone for the holidays, sicknesses going around, and Tyler being home, the two of them had buddied up quite a bit during their down time. But school had restarted along with dance, and Hannah had been spending more time with friends on weekends. Nicole had seen Abby cuddled up with her tablet more often during the past two weeks and didn't like it. But it was cold outside, she'd finished all her new books, and one could play alone only for so long. Nicole couldn't blame her for being bored. Add to that, Hannah's dance competitions were starting back up and would occupy at least two weekends each month through the spring. It was all but guaranteed that Abby would be having more tablet time in the car and in between the sets. Nicole sighed. She and Sam had decided that if they made any changes to dance, it would be over the summer when there was a natural break, but Nicole felt like she was already primed to throw in the towel.

And then there was the promotion.

Nicole felt her heart pound and a jolt of anxiety rushed through her limbs.

The entire situation was a mess.

She and Sam had talked it over and decided that there was no commitment in applying. Sam could always turn down the job if it was offered to him, but he couldn't have the choice unless he took that initial step.

If he was offered the promotion and took it, the money would be excellent. There was no downside, as far as that was concerned. Better pay, higher status in the company, the possibility of a company car, yearly bonus trips. The list went on. A year ago, she doubted he would have even asked for her approval. He would simply have taken it, assuming that she'd be on board with whatever gave them a higher class of living.

But now things were different. The job had a definite cost to its promises of financial blessing. Sam would have to be away more, often for a week at a time. He'd have to do a lot more driving and work more hours. More conferences. More meetings. More time on his phone. And there was even a possibility that they'd eventually have to relocate to a bigger city so that he was more accessible to the corporate office.

Nicole piled silverware into the dishwasher and swallowed the lump rising in her throat. If Sam took the job, it was all but inevitable they'd go backward. All the progress they'd made, all the connections they had worked to establish, would all go up in a puff of smoke. She was sure of it. Nicole mostly hoped that somehow, they'd offer the position to someone else. Sam would be hurt, but he also wouldn't be forced to make a difficult choice. Nicole tried to keep her feelings to herself, but the truth was, she desperately wanted Sam to turn down the job. *But I can't tell him that. He'd resent me.*

And if he took it, she'd probably resent him.

It had to be his decision. She couldn't turn it down for him, much as she'd like to. And so, she prayed.

Nicole closed the dishwasher and tapped the start button twice. Christmas had given them all a glimpse of what their home could be like if they kept things simple, but life was roaring back into their faces with a vengeance and like it or not, they had decisions to make.

***

"You're going to love this place." Wyatt met them at the door of Brad's Burgers and Brew and held it open as the Richardsons filed through. He clapped Tyler on the shoulder. "The burgers are as big as your head."

Nicole brought up the rear as her family filed into the restaurant and made their way to a large corner table to join the Millers. Menus with the restaurant's name splashed across the covers sat waiting at each seat, a glass of ice water already available for each patron.

"Wow, good service. We weren't even here, and they had drinks ready." Kyle plopped into a chair and stretched. "Ahhh, no second chair needed for the leg. It's the simple things."

The Millers already had sodas in front of them, and their menus were closed. Nicole slid into the chair across from Jessica and frowned. "Are we late? Have you guys been waiting long?"

"No, not at all." Jessica twirled her straw in her glass and pulled a cherry from her Roy Rogers. "They know us because this was where Wyatt worked in high school, so they set us up."

"Don't all the proceeds from today go toward the Mexico trip for Grace's youth group?" Sam unzipped his coat and flung it over the back of his chair. "I meant to put it on my calendar and forgot."

Tom grinned. "Yeah, the owner goes to our church and does this whenever there's an upcoming trip, usually every year or two."

Nicole raised her eyebrows. "Oh, wow."

Tom took a sip of his Coca-Cola. "Yeah, it's super generous." He smiled as he watched the seven kids chat happily at the table, oblivious to their parents. "Think they've forgotten we're here?"

"Until the bill arrives, probably," Sam said. Tom laughed.

"How'd the assignment from last time go?" Jessica asked.

"Good," Sam said. "The handout you sent home with Nicole was more helpful than I expected. It helped keep us focused on our family vision while we were working through things."

"I really enjoyed the process," Nicole said. "Especially when we brought the kids into it. Discussing things with them has been a game changer for me. I don't feel nearly as lost." She let out a small laugh. "Go figure. Actually talking to your kids can offer a lot of clarity. I feel like that's such an obvious thing. I don't even think I realized how much I wasn't checking in with them before going through this with you guys."

"Well, if it isn't one of my favorite families!" A booming voice broke into their conversation, and Nicole looked up to see a tall, thick-set man striding toward their table with a wide smile stretched across his face. The ceiling lights bounced brightly off his completely bald head. He had to be well over six feet tall and looked as solid as a block of cement, but his eyes twinkled in genuine happiness as he shook hands with Tom and clapped a hand as big as a ham on Wyatt's shoulder.

"Hey, Brad!" Tom was positively dwarfed next to Wyatt's old employer, and Nicole bit back a smile. "You knew we couldn't miss today."

"Looks like a lot of other people felt the same way," Brad said, sweeping his hand toward the very full dining area. "Should be good for the Mexico trip."

"Absolutely. Have you met the Richardsons? They're new to Grace." Tom introduced each of them in turn, and Brad shook hands with Sam and Nicole.

"Good to meet all of you." Brad nodded toward the menus in front of them. "I think Jayna is your waitress today, and she's a gem, so you'll be in good hands." He flashed his smile again. "Want me to send out baskets of fries to get you started?"

"You know us well," Tom said with a laugh. "That would be great, thanks."

Brad winked at the teenagers at the other end of the table. "I know the drill. How many sauces do you guys want besides ketchup?"

"Oh, they have the best fry sauce," Whitney said. "Can we get that and ranch?"

"You got it." Brad waved as he stepped away from the table. "Good to see you guys. Enjoy dinner!"

Nicole watched him leave, the waiters and waitresses parting in front of him like some strange version of the Red Sea. "How tall is he?"

"Six foot six," Wyatt said. "Brad's awesome. He was my first boss, and I'm pretty sure I've been spoiled for life."

Tom rubbed his hands together. "Brad's an incredible employer and has an excellent mind for business. That's actually one reason we picked this location for this week's topic. Well, that and the chance to help with the missions trip."

"Two birds, one stone," Sam said. "Makes sense."

"Exactly." Tom took another gulp from his glass. "The theme of this week is Taking Action. But before we get into it, we have a little assignment for you."

Jessica tapped her menu. "I think we should probably look over these first so we're ready to order, Tom."

"Perfect." Tom turned his attention back to Sam and Nicole. "They're expecting to be very busy today, so we want you to observe the flow of the restaurant: what the workers are doing, where Brad turns his attention, how the customers are reacting to the service..." His voice trailed off. "Stuff like that. And then we can discuss what you've noticed later."

Nicole flipped open her menu. "Sounds good." Her eyes scanned the pages in front of her. "Any recommendations?"

"Anything," Jessica said. "You won't be disappointed."

***

"That may have been the best burger I've had in Devon Falls," Sam said, sitting back in his chair and letting out a low groan. "I never thought I'd say this, but I think I actually ate too much."

Nicole stared at her own plate, the last third of her chicken sandwich still uneaten. "I'm taking mine home."

"Oh, I never finish my dinner when we eat here." Jessica pulled a packet of wipes out of her purse and cleaned off her hands. She passed the wipes to Whitney and told her to take one and pass it down.

"So, what did you notice about how this restaurant runs?" Tom asked. He glanced down the table and addressed the four Richardson kids. "Did you guys hear me tell your parents what to look out for?" They all nodded. "Okay, so if you noticed anything, I want to hear from you too."

Nicole glanced over in surprise at Abby's voice. "Well, they were really fast." She looked shyly at Tom. "Usually when we go out to eat, we have to wait a long time if it's busy, but not here."

"That's true." Nicole had noticed the same thing. "This place runs like a well-oiled machine."

"The food was excellent." Sam gestured to his empty plate. "Obviously."

"They were helping each other." That was the thing that had interested Nicole the most. "I saw a guy offer to help one of the girls with a particularly full tray of drinks. And one of the girls helped serve a table that wasn't hers."

"I was surprised how active Brad is in this whole thing." Sam leaned forward and rested his forearms on the edge of the table. "He's the boss and the owner, so he could technically just bark orders and expect they be followed. But he was in the thick of it with his employees instead, making sure his workers had what they needed and checking on the customers."

"Oh yeah, he knows *everyone*," Wyatt said. "He's got an incredible memory when it comes to names and faces. If you guys come back, he'll probably know all of you on sight."

"I'm just amazed everything is running so smoothly when it's this busy," Nicole said.

Tyler cocked his head. "They operate more like a team than a bunch of individuals just coming into work. I mean, not everyone is doing the same job, but it's like they're all committed to a very specific way the day needs to go." He shrugged. "Reminds me of sports."

"That's a great observation," Tom said. "And I think Wyatt would agree that Brad purposely sets up his staff to act as a team." He looked at his son. "Is that true?"

Wyatt nodded. "Yeah, he really does. Our schedule was always very specific and predictable, so we knew exactly what was expected of us. And then if we made certain goals for the month, we got bonuses—smaller ones for individuals and bigger ones for everyone to split, so the workers make a point to cheer each other on toward them."

Tom pointed a fry at Sam. "So, you'd be Brad in your family situation, right? The responsibility of how your family is operating ultimately falls to you as head of household, biblically speaking." He gestured to Nicole. "Though Nicole is a huge part of this too. While Brad is both the owner and the manager of this place, in a family it's a little different."

Sam nodded. "I could see the parallel. The dad is kind of like the owner. He's on the hook for how things go, but also delegates to whoever he hires as a manager." He winked at Nicole. "That's you."

"Yes, and even though the manager does a lot of the hands-on work, they have to be in lockstep with the owner and make decisions in tandem with him," Jessica said.

"In a family, your vision statement is a huge help here," Tom said. "It's much easier to raise children when you're united in a goal." He reached for another fry. "This restaurant wouldn't run nearly as smoothly if the staff wasn't focused on one thing: getting good food to their customers in a timely manner. If the cooks in the back were more interested in socializing or the waiters didn't care about how fast they got to their tables, the rhythm of the entire place would change or shut down. The same holds true for families. If you have different goals, you'll parent at cross-purposes and that makes things difficult."

Nicole took a sip of Dr. Pepper and fiddled with her fork.

"So, taking action means to make sure we're united?" It seemed redundant.

"Nah, it's just the thing that has to be in place for the action to happen," Tom assured her. "The action has to do with choosing to get rid of things that are not helping you move toward your family vision, and adding or tweaking things that will."

"Fine-tuning," Sam summarized.

"Yes, and that's where your homework will be focused." Tom pulled out his phone. "Do you guys have a family calendar?"

"I keep one in the kitchen," Nicole said. "Honestly, it's mostly for me."

"Do you use that too, Sam?"

Sam shook his head. "Not really. I use the calendar on my phone, and it's for work."

Tom opened an app on his phone. "Okay, so there are several good options out there, but we really like this one. It's a family calendar and you can link up your lines so that everyone has access to it."

Sam didn't look convinced. "I can't really have my work schedule on our personal calendar. I'm sure there would be some sort of confidentiality issue if I did that."

Tom waved his hand in dismissal. "No, nothing like that. All your work information should stay as it is." He tapped his phone. "But anything family related—doctor's appointments, days you're on call, dance practices, school events—they should all be in one place where everyone can access the information. Putting the life of your family all in one place will allow you to see what activities are planned into your weekly and monthly schedules and can give you needed perspective."

"I have the app on my phone, but usually I copy everything onto our paper calendar at home," Jessica said. "The app is nice for when I'm out and about, but I personally prefer a hard copy."

Tom smirked. "She's old."

"Point being, both formats have their merits." Jessica elbowed her husband playfully in the ribs. "And here's a tip: Go over the calendar once a week. We do ours on Sunday nights. It makes things so much easier when the entire family is entering the week knowing what's coming up." She gave Will a small smile. "And then no one can claim they weren't told about an event."

Will made a face. "Hey, that hasn't happened in a while!"

Hannah giggled and covered her mouth.

"I don't know about you, but seeing my week at a glance can be a really helpful visual to determine if we're too busy or if something specific is taking up more time than it should," Jessica said. "Or it might show us what's missing."

Tom nodded in agreement. "For us, we tend to start with our most important priorities first, get them on the calendar, and then see if we have space for extra activities." He ran through a list. "Church events, important appointments, family dinners, stuff like that comes first. Then the extracurriculars and bonus activities are written in after that."

Nicole shifted in her seat and shot a look down the table at Hannah, who was chatting happily with Will. "I have a feeling that dance is going to dominate our calendar when I write in all of Hannah's practices and competitions."

Jessica cocked her head. "You mentioned on the phone last week that you were feeling really burned out with it. Have you thought about paring down?"

Nicole sighed. "We want to, but we also understand that because she's already made some commitments for this spring, any changes won't just affect her but her whole team, and we didn't feel like that was fair. We thought it would be best to make any changes during the summer." She rested her chin in her palm and lowered her voice. "We already know we're going to have her take the summer off. We just don't know what restarting in the fall will look like. And she doesn't know any of this yet."

Sam rolled his eyes. "You'll know when we tell her. I'm sure the screams will travel to your house."

Tom laughed and nodded. "Okay, is there anything else you two feel should be taken off your schedule or reduced? Or is Hannah's dance the only thing?"

Sam sat back in his chair. "Actually, yeah. My being on call."

Nicole looked at her husband in surprise. "What?"

"I've been thinking about it lately," Sam said. "Everyone in my company is required to be on call once every six weeks, either Saturday or Sunday. I'm on the Sunday rotation." He cleared his throat. "But I've gotten into the habit of picking up an extra weekend or two during those six-week chunks because the money's so good. It usually isn't hard picking up more shifts, since most guys would rather be completely off on the weekends." He looked thoughtful. "We've been trying to attend church as a family as often as possible, and now it's cutting into that in a way I don't like. I think I should back off and just take the one shift I'm assigned without picking up any more." He gave Nicole a half-smile. "I assume you'd be okay with that."

"Um, yes," Nicole said, delight evident in the two words.

"Speaking of church attendance, how are your other spiritual routines going?" Tom asked.

"Pretty good. She's better than me," Sam said, pointing at Nicole. "I'd say I get mine in about four times a week. She does it almost every day."

"But you've been listening to that audio Bible app in your truck a lot," Nicole pointed out. "That still counts."

Sam looked doubtful. "Maybe."

"It totally counts," Jessica said. "You might not feel as focused, but you're still filling your mind with truth and becoming more familiar with Scripture." She grinned. "Have you guys put any other routines in place?"

"We're kind of failing at family worship," Nicole said. "It's been really hard to sit down with the kids and do it. Hannah gets home so late that she basically eats supper and then heads to her room to do homework."

Tom looked thoughtful. "Can I make a suggestion?"

"Please."

"Have the kids bring their Bibles to supper and put them under their chairs. When you're done eating, just tack it onto the end of the meal." He pointed at his own children. "Family worship is something we did even before we took the class and this strategy worked well for us. We also kept a little bag of chocolate chips or mini marshmallows nearby when the kids were little. They would each get five at the end of supper to eat while we read our Bible together." He smiled at the memory. "It made the time something they looked forward to, and we would often remind them that God's Word is 'sweet' to us."

"Oh, I like that!" Though Nicole doubted that chocolate chips or marshmallows would entice her teenagers, a simple dessert might be a good option. Plus, Hannah had been wanting to bake more ever since Christmas. Maybe she could have her make some cookie dough to freeze.

"I've been reading with Abby most nights," Sam said. "Not her Bible, just a chapter book." He shrugged. "Not exactly a spiritual discipline."

"You're still building memories with your daughter. That definitely has a spiritual component and helps put into practice your family vision," Tom said. "Has it been going well?"

"Yeah. We're in the middle of *Matilda*."

"That's great," Jessica said. "Father-daughter time is super special. And you're already getting good time with Tyler and Kyle in the basement." She looked at Nicole. "How about time with Hannah?"

Nicole shook her head.

"Dance," Jessica said.

"Yes." Nicole shrugged. "It really is cramping my style, but I want to finish what we started. Things should die down at the end of May."

"So that's it?" Sam looked between the two of them. "You want us to make a calendar and plug our schedule and routines into it and see what needs to change?"

"That's most of it," Tom acknowledged. "And then the other part is budgeting."

"We already have a budget," Nicole said.

"Good, then this should be easy." Tom shoved his phone back into his pocket. "I'm sure your budget is mostly focused on your monthly expenses, right?"

"Sure."

"As you guys take into consideration your parenting plan, it's important to look at how it could affect your future," Tom said. "For new parents, that might mean starting to save up for homeschooling curriculum or private school tuition long before their kids need it. For you guys, it might be the expenses of school activities or next year's tuition, a missions trip coming up over the summer, or a family vacation." He grinned. "Some of the goals will be for the short term, in a year or two. But other goals might be a little farther out. It's good to have them in mind so that you can make wise decisions with your money now."

"If you have a financial advisor, they can be great about helping you set goals and plans," Jessica said. "And we'd encourage you guys to include giving in this process too. I mean, everything we have is God's anyway, right?" She spread her hands. "Saving to give is a great way to build generosity into your life."

Tom laced his fingers together loosely. "So that's the homework. Get your family calendar going and figure out if you need to make any adjustments, either taking things off your schedule or adding some stuff in as you see fit." He smiled. "Then, pray about it and commit to it. Once you've kept it going for a few weeks, feel free to celebrate! It's a big accomplishment to stay the course."

"And then review our budget with our finance guy," Sam said.

"Well, review your budget together for sure," Tom said. "And if you have a financial advisor, it might be a good idea to connect with him if you haven't in a while."

"I think it's been over a year." Nicole frowned, trying to remember. "I'm not sure, I'd have to call and ask."

"Hey!" Kyle's voice interrupted her thoughts as he waved his hand at them from the other end of the table, a dessert menu in his hand. "I have requests!"

"How can you eat after this?" Nicole was incredulous.

Tyler shrugged. "Not to put too fine a point on it, but I could go for something sweet too."

Nicole shook her head and laughed as Sam beckoned for the menu. "All right. Let's see what magic they can work with chocolate."

LESSON 5:

Action - Learn how to successfully implement your plan.

CHAPTER 10

"**Y**ou guys have a minute?"

Nicole looked up from her book as Tyler walked into their bedroom. Sam finished tugging a clean t-shirt over his head and picked up the remote, hitting mute on the basketball game flickering over the screen. "Sure, what's up?"

Tyler's eyes darted from his dad to the TV, then to Nicole.

"Can we turn the game off for a few minutes, Sam?"

"Huh? Oh." Sam took the hint, and the screen went black. He glanced at Tyler. "Everything okay?"

"Yeah, everything's fine." Tyler shifted from one foot to the other, clearly uncomfortable. "I just wanted to run something by you."

Sam sat down on the side of the bed. "Shoot."

Tyler squared his shoulders and swallowed. Nicole felt alarm rise in her chest. Had he been drinking again? *Please no.* She'd thought he'd been doing better once he'd gone back to school two weeks ago, but maybe she was the stereotypical out-of-touch mom in denial. *Oh God, whatever it is, please keep us calm.*

"First, I want to say that I really appreciate all you guys have done for me in college so far this year." The words were measured, rehearsed. He had clearly planned this. "I know I got a scholarship, but tuition isn't cheap, and I get that."

Sam was silent. Nicole could see a frown forming at the corners of his eyes. They were both waiting for the bad news.

"I was wondering if you would both be okay—" Tyler blew out a breath and drummed his thumbs on his thighs. "I was wondering if you'd be okay with me dropping out of football."

Stunned silence filled the room.

Nicole was the first to recover. "Tyler—" She watched Sam in her peripheral vision. "I mean, we'd never force you to play if you really didn't want to." Relief trickled down her limbs. Was this it? Was this what he was so nervous to share?

But Tyler's eyes were on Sam. "Dad?"

Sam blinked. The frown Nicole had seen forming becoming more pronounced. "Why? Why would you want to quit?"

Tyler crossed his arms over his chest. "I just do."

"Tyler, you can be honest with us. Did something else happen?"

Tyler ran a hand through his hair and grimaced. "Not exactly."

Sam crossed his own arms and leaned back on the headboard. "'Not exactly' and 'no' aren't the same thing. Spill it."

"I didn't do anything, I swear." Tyler's eyes widened in earnest. "You don't know what it's like! All the guys on the team drink every weekend. *Every weekend*. And they invite me. Since I went back to school, I've told them no twice."

"Well, you've been coming home every weekend," Sam said.

Tyler looked at his father in exasperation. "Guess why."

Nicole dropped her book onto the covers in realization. "To get away from the temptation."

"Yes." Tyler clenched his jaw. "Seriously, Mom, I don't want to do that stuff."

Sam's face softened. He cleared his throat. "You've been coming home so you aren't tempted to drink?"

Tyler rubbed a hand down his face. "I love football. I do. But college football is totally different than football at Heritage." He shook his head. "In high school, my coach was a Christian, and most of the guys on my team went to church." He paused. "I'm the only Christian on the team that I know."

"How about the coach?"

Tyler gave a sardonic laugh. "With his mouth? Doubt it." He was silent for a moment. "And the truth is, I'm nothing special."

"Tyler, that's not true." Sam was shaking his head.

Tyler spread his hands. "I know I'm a good football player, okay? But at Heritage, I was a big fish in a little pond. At Western, I'm average. I'm never going to be the star of the team. I know what talent is and some of these guys are incredible."

Nicole watched Sam. She knew he was struggling between two warring emotions: Pride at the strength their son was showing by trying to remove himself from a bad situation, and sadness that a special time in his life was apparently ending.

She kept her voice soft. "I know this is a tough choice for you."

"Not as much as you'd think." Tyler's eyes strayed to Sam again, and he dropped his gaze. "I miss what football was for me in high school, but I can't get that back. Honestly the hardest part was knowing that you guys might be disappointed in me for quitting." He swallowed hard. "I just don't think I can hang around those guys and not be stupid."

Nicole felt tears gather in her eyes. "Honey—"

But then Sam was on his feet, wrapping Tyler in a bear hug. Tyler almost lost his balance in surprise and Sam pulled back, gripping his shoulders. "There is zero disappointment for your mother and me." He looked hard at Tyler, as if he could drill the truth of his words deep into his son's brain. "I'm serious. What we are is proud of you."

Tears spilled onto Nicole's cheeks. She dabbed at them discreetly with her sleeve.

"Mom, don't cry."

"I'm fine!" *Thank you, Lord.*

Sam released Tyler with a grin and clapped him on the back.

"There's one more thing." Tyler looked relieved, the tension in his face slowly ebbing away. "And I haven't made any decisions yet, but I want your feedback."

"Okay." Sam sat back down on the bed and laced his fingers together. "What about?"

"School next year." Tyler hooked his thumbs through his belt loops. "I started college not knowing what I wanted to do for a career."

Nicole nodded. "That's normal."

"Yeah, I know. But I think I might have an idea now." He gave a small smile.

There was a pause.

Sam quirked an eyebrow. "Are you trying to keep us in suspense?"

"Maybe a little." Tyler jerked his head toward their door. "It was working on the basement that helped me figure it out."

Sam looked surprised. "Which part?"

Tyler raised his shoulders in a shrug. "Lots of it, but mostly the electrical work. What you do." He grinned. "I don't know. It just makes sense to me. I could totally see myself doing that as a career."

Nicole bit back a smile.

Sam looked completely shocked. "Are you serious?"

"Completely. Which is why—" Tyler looked between them. "I'd like to know what you'd think about my changing to the trade school Wyatt goes to. Don't worry, I'll finish out the year at Western. But they have an awesome electrician apprenticeship program. It's supposed to be one of the best in the state."

Sam raised his eyebrows and said nothing.

Nicole held up a finger. "Can I mention something?"

"Sure."

"One difficult thing about that," She looked between her husband and son. "You might try it out and discover that you actually don't want to go the same route as your dad." She put a hand on Sam's arm. "And that's okay, but it also means that if you want to go back to Western, you'll have lost your academic scholarship. I'm not saying it's a bad idea, I just want to make sure you understand that there is some finality if you do this. Dad and I can't afford to send you back to that school without financial aid."

Tyler nodded. "I know. And I haven't made any decisions yet, I just wanted to see if you guys were open to me exploring it." His eyes darted between his parents. "Which you are, right?"

Nicole looked at Sam, who quirked a smile. "You want to follow in my footsteps and save me money? Don't expect me to fight you."

Tyler let out a small laugh.

"But your mom is right," Sam said. "This isn't a decision you want to make lightly, so make sure you think it through. Let's talk about it some more tomorrow when we're working downstairs?"

"Yeah, sounds good. Thanks." Tyler gave a wide smile, relief evident all over his face. He walked to the doorway and tapped the frame. "Night. Love you guys." He shut their door on his way out, leaving Sam and Nicole in a comfortable silence.

Nicole reached for her book again and rifled back through the pages to find her place. "Well, that was a conversation I never thought we'd have."

"No kidding." Sam gazed at the doorway with a befuddled expression on his face. "Go figure," he said, more to himself than anyone else.

Nicole found her place and spread the book open. "If only Hannah could come to the same conclusion about dance."

Sam let out a bark of a laugh. "Fat chance."

"I know." They'd sat Hannah down earlier in the week and told her that she and Abby would be taking the summer off. It had gone about as well as they'd expected, though Nicole had been glad that there had been more tears than screaming. Abby had been disappointed but gotten over it quickly. Hannah, however, was still moping.

"Today I told Heather we were taking the summer off since we carpool so much. You know, just as a courtesy."

Sam picked up the remote and turned the game back on. "Probably a good call."

"Well, she certainly doesn't think so."

"What?" Sam muted the TV and turned to her in surprise. "Why is it her business what we choose to do with Hannah?"

Nicole pinched the bridge of her nose. "I think she thought I was making a judgment. I was telling her how we're trying to connect more as a family and be more intentional in our parenting, and she took it personally."

"You mean like you were telling her what to do?"

"Our families have always done a lot of the same things with the kids," Nicole said. "I think she felt like I was telling her that if she didn't do what we are, she's doing something wrong."

"But that's not what you said."

"No, but I think that's what she heard."

Sam leaned back into his pillow. "Well, that's dumb."

Nicole let out a sad laugh. "Agreed."

"We should be able to make family decisions for ourselves without other people taking it personally," Sam said, shaking his head.

"I'm just telling you what I *think* she was thinking. I could be wrong." Nicole sighed. "The truth is, I don't want to live the weekend-competition life anymore, and I don't think it's best for the girls." She squirmed. "Honestly, I don't think it's best for Kara or Paisley or any of the other girls either, but they're not my kids. We're responsible for Hannah and Abby."

"Yep." Sam's eyes strayed back to the basketball game.

She'd said enough. Nicole snuggled deeper into the covers and drew her book closer. Parenting was not an easy journey. When she and Sam had started this process, she hadn't considered that it might affect relationships outside of their family as well. Heather was a good friend. She'd hate to think that this would cause distance between them.

Then again, choices had consequences. And if forced to pick between her old life and the new one they were trying to forge, Nicole knew which one she'd choose.

***

"Oh, that's tough."

Jessica gave Nicole a look of compassion and cringed. "Have you talked to Heather since then?"

"Just in passing." Nicole sighed and gave a sad smile. "Is this how it's going to be? Our choices offending people who have always been our friends? I don't feel like it should be this big of a deal."

Jessica waved to Tom and Sam, who stood at the entrance to the hospital's cafeteria. Tom was just ending a shift, and they were all meeting to go out to dinner. "You're right that it shouldn't be, as it doesn't affect anyone but you guys." She slipped her arm around Tom's waist as he joined them. "But sometimes people feel judged simply because you're making different decisions than they are, and that's not your fault."

Sam eyed Nicole. "Sharing your Heather struggles?"

"Yes."

"I won't lie. It certainly helps to have a group of people who are like-minded around you when it comes to parenting," Jessica said. "Like all the families at the coffeehouse, remember?"

"We can go to those, right?" Nicole asked.

"Oh, for sure. We've gotten close to several families who attend, and we've been able to support each other as we all implement our parenting plans and tweak things as the kids grow."

"Speaking of the parenting plan, how has it been going?" Tom rubbed the back of his neck. He looked tired.

"Sam didn't sign up for any extra on-call shifts, so we've been able to all be at church the past two weeks," Nicole said, warmth flooding her chest. Being in church every week with Sam was something she didn't take for granted. "And we've been doing family worship after dinner. It's way easier to implement when everyone always has their stuff." She squeezed Sam's hand. "Hannah misses more than I'd like because her practices have been running late, but we've been making an effort to connect with her over dinner even if we've already eaten." It wasn't ideal, but it was something. Nicole was hopeful that when dance died down, Hannah would appreciate being at home for dinner every night.

Tom gave an encouraging smile. "We wanted to tell you guys how much of a privilege it's been to go through this with you. You've done a lot of work."

"Believe it or not, this is our final formal lesson. Though of course, we'd still love to get together as friends," Jessica said.

Sam crossed his arms. "So does this mean we don't have homework this week?"

Tom laughed. "Not officially. Just some friendly direction." He pointed at a wall of photos on one side of the cafeteria. "Let's head this way."

Jessica hooked her arm through Nicole's as they made their way to the other side of the room. "Today's all about Reviewing and Revising, and we've already kind of touched on what that means." Jessica tucked a strand of blonde hair behind her ear. "It's important that as you continue in your parenting journey, that you make connections with other couples who are living a similar life so you can support each other. And of course, it's a good idea for you and Sam to periodically review your family vision and parenting plan. Your kids are going to continue to grow and change and without revisiting your vision and plan, it's easy to get off track."

Tom nodded, stopping beside a wall filled with several framed photographs. "We like to review ours during road trips actually. Since everyone is in the car together for several hours, there's plenty of time for us to discuss things as a couple and get input from the kids as needed. Now—" He tapped the wall with an open palm. "This is the History Wall."

Nicole looked at the photo next to him, a grainy, faded portrait of the hospital when it first opened some forty years before. "Why is it in the cafeteria?" She would have expected something like this to be in a lobby or corridor, not the place where workers took their breaks and ate during their shifts.

"It used to be in the entryway, but about ten years ago they moved the display in here."

Tom gazed at the wall affectionately. "The board decided to put it here as a reminder to the workers."

"Reminder of what?" Sam frowned in confusion.

"The doctors and nurses and staff who have gone before us. Almost all the people who were here when the place was built have retired or passed away. In another forty years, all of us will be gone and there will be a new crop of medical professionals dedicated to the community of Devon Falls." Tom looked between them, explaining. "This wall is seen by everyone who works here, from the new college kid doing inventory to the most seasoned surgeon. It's meant to help us remember that we are a part of something special that is much bigger than any of us."

Nicole's eyes roamed the photos on the wall with new interest. "That's really sweet."

Tom nodded. "I wanted you to see the differences in each photograph. Look at all the changes." He pointed to the second picture on the wall. "This one was taken five years after the hospital was built, and there isn't a huge difference. But the next one—" He moved his finger over to the third photo. "This is when the east wing was expanded to include a bigger surgical department."

"I remember that," Sam said. "I was Hannah's age when that went up. It was a big deal for the town."

"Yep. It meant that we didn't have to outsource to bigger hospitals as much," Tom said. He nodded toward the rest of the pictures. "If you keep going, you'll end up seeing the picture that was taken about three years ago at the end. When you compare it to the original building, it's amazing how different it looks. But most of the changes occurred a bit at a time and aren't very noticeable if you only compare pictures that are right next to each other."

Sam nudged Nicole and grinned. "I sense a metaphor."

Jessica laughed. "He knows us well."

Tom chuckled. "Over the years, things at this hospital have changed. In a similar way, you both have changed over the years and even in the past several weeks." He motioned to Nicole. "I doubt your days look much like they did twelve years ago when you had three small children and no teenagers. You've adapted, grown, and made changes."

Nicole nodded. "Back when Tyler was little, tablets weren't really a thing, and most kids didn't have phones. We're dealing with technology in a very different way with Abby."

"Makes sense," Jessica said.

"Some things changed for us in a negative way," Tom said. "We were very intentional when the kids were small to teach them doctrine and Bible stories, but when they entered school, we backed off because they were getting it at Heritage." He gave a half smile. "And then we were convicted about that and started being intentional again a few years later." He pointed to an older man standing in the cafeteria line. His white doctor's coat was newly pressed.

"That's Dr. Patrick," Tom said. "He's the only staff member I know of who has been working at this hospital since day one. Granted, he's sixty-nine and only comes in twice a week, but he's an incredible surgeon and a bona fide original."

"Really?" Nicole watched the older man reach for a slice of cherry pie.

"He's fascinating to talk to," Tom said. "He remembers when every building addition went up, every new surgical procedure was tested. He knows when they started putting robots into the operating rooms." He laughed. "He told me that was the day he knew The Jetsons would one day be real."

Sam cracked a smile. "I bet his surgical practices have changed too."

"For sure. New techniques, mastering tried-and-true ones, learning from colleagues and conferences, and even inventing some of his own methods. I wouldn't be surprised if one day they name a new wing after him or something." Tom looked at Dr. Patrick in admiration. "I assume you understand what I'm trying to say."

"It's much like parenting," Sam summarized. "We'll try new things, master others, and figure out what works for our unique situation."

"And it's important to revisit your parenting plan on the regular. Consider it to be continuing ed," Tom said.

Jessica folded her arms across her chest and sighed. "I can't believe this is our last official lesson with you guys. The time really seemed to fly by, at least for me."

"It has been fast," Nicole agreed. "I'm thankful we'll still see you at church and can get together for fun sometimes." She turned and looked at the nearby table where all seven kids were passing the time playing a few rounds of Five Crowns. "I'm thankful for the sweet friendships they've been able to rekindle."

"Us too," Jessica said. "And we're always available to talk about this stuff. Just because we're technically finished with our mentor relationship doesn't mean we can't keep this conversation going."

"We're planning to attend those quarterly parenting discussions," Sam said. "I think that will be a big support."

"Absolutely. And at one point, you guys will probably meet a couple who has similar struggles and could benefit from this class, so feel free to tell them about it. Think of it as a way to pay it forward by directing others." Tom grinned. "Who knows, you two might end up as a mentor couple sometime!"

Jessica gave Tom a playful shove. "Don't pressure them."

Tom held up his hands in surrender. "No pressure. Just mentioning it."

"Mentoring *is* fun," Jessica said. "And it has good benefits. I always end up feeling like we become better parents when we go through this with another family because the reminders help us uncover blind spots and things we need to change even now."

"You guys have blind spots?" Sam cocked an eyebrow. "I thought you were pretty much perfect."

Tom laughed. "You should have seen us arguing this morning. We're far from perfect."

Jessica wrinkled her nose. "I had to call him and apologize."

"Which I accepted, and then gave my own," Tom said. "But yes, we still have blind spots. These meetings have helped your family, but they've been a real blessing to us too."

"Like that proverb," Nicole said. "'As iron sharpens iron, so one man sharpens another.'"

"Proverbs 27:17," Tom said. "One of my favorites."

Jessica slid her purse higher up on her shoulder and looked across the cafeteria at the kids. "Should be we going? It would be nice to beat the dinner rush."

"Sounds good to me," Sam said, slipping Nicole's hand into his. "Where are we going?"

Tom grinned and pointed at Abby. "Tradition says that the youngest member of the mentee family gets to decide the celebration dinner."

Nicole laughed. "Then prepare for pizza."

* * *

Today was the day.

Nicole's hand shook slightly as she poured herself a second mug of coffee and sat down on one of the bar stools across from Sam. She'd helped him pick out the right outfit for his interview, and she admired him across the island: navy blue slacks, a button-down shirt, black shoes. His tie hung over his shoulders, still needing to be tied, but that was the last step before he headed out the door.

"How do I look?"

"Sharp. Navy's a good color on you." Nicole ran her fingers over a page in her Bible absentmindedly. She'd gotten up extra early today—sleep had been hard to come by—and spent the last hour reading and praying.

When Sam had come out of their room, she'd paused to cook him some eggs and toast. "Are you nervous?"

"Not really." Sam stuck a final forkful of eggs into his mouth and turned to set his dish into the sink. "They know me. They know what they want for the company. Whatever happens, it'll be fine."

Nicole sipped her coffee as her stomach did backflips. She was glad that his appetite didn't seem to be affected by the possibility of big changes for their family. Hers on the other hand...

"You okay?"

"I guess." She had never been good at hiding things from Sam. "Just nervous for you."

Sam gave her a confident smile. "Don't worry. I've got this."

Which is exactly what she was afraid of.

Nicole stared into the depths of her mug. Sam was probably a shoo-in for the promotion, or at least a top contender. And while the job would be a huge boost to his career, Nicole couldn't shake the feeling that it would take their family in the completely wrong direction.

"Kids not up yet?"

"Hannah's in the shower, but Kyle and Abby are still asleep." The kids didn't know about the possible job change. Sam and Nicole had agreed that it was best not to tell them until something was set in stone.

Both of their phones pinged in unison.

Praying for you guys today. Love ya.

Nicole felt the corners of her mouth turn up. They had explained the situation to Tyler last weekend so that he could be prepared for any changes this might bring. They'd also asked him to pray for them, which he apparently had taken to heart.

Nicole sent back a quick text. *Thanks, Ty. Love you 2.* She looked at Sam. "Tyler's praying."

"For which I'm thankful." Sam grabbed his tie and twisted it into a proper knot. "I'll call when I'm done, okay? Should be around nine."

"I'll make sure my phone is on." Nicole slid off the bar stool and walked to the sink, emptying the last half of her mug. "I should be home by then."

Sam checked his watch and grabbed his coat off the back of a chair. "I want to get some paperwork done before they call me back, so I'm going to head out. Is my tie okay?"

"Almost perfect." Nicole tugged the edges of the knot to smooth them and playfully tugged the bottom of the tie. "Knock 'em dead."

Sam grinned, gave her a quick kiss and a hug, then turned and disappeared into the garage.

She could hear the bay door opening and the start of Sam's pickup. A minute later, the sound of his motor died away and the grinding of the gears signaled that the garage was closing again. Nicole took a deep breath and swallowed, her eyes roaming over the kitchen as a pit settled in her stomach.

God was in control.

It was the truth she clung to.

LESSON 6:

Review and Revise - Incorporate ways to review your plan and progress on a regular basis and make changes to that plan as needed.

LESSON 7:

Direct Others - When your family is on a clear and focused path, you will be blessed and also be a blessing to others by helping other families who may be struggling on their Christian family journey.

EPILOGUE

Six months later

"That smells incredible."

Sam's compliment made Nicole smile as she pulled a piping hot lasagna out of the oven. Mozzarella cheese bubbled on top, and she carefully set the Pyrex on top of a cooling rack. "Still got it."

"You never lost it, babe."

Nicole laughed and glanced at the clock. "Oh! They're going to be here any second. Can you make sure that Abby picked up her socks in the basement? I swear there's a new pair on the floor whenever I go down there."

"She's still downstairs. I'll call down." Sam walked over to the open basement door. "Abs, make sure you bring up your socks!"

Abby's voice drifted back upstairs, but Nicole couldn't make out her reply. She pulled the salad Hannah had made out of the fridge and set it on the counter, then lifted three bottles of dressing from the door. All she had left to add was croutons.

The doorbell rang.

"They're here!" Nicole could hear the excitement in Hannah's voice as she bounded to the front door and swung it open with a wide smile. "Hi, you guys!"

The Millers had arrived.

A chorus of happy voices filled the entryway, and Nicole felt herself grin. It had been over two months since their families had seen each other outside of church, and now that school had restarted, she and Jessica had finally both settled into routines and picked a night for everyone to catch up.

Jessica wandered into the kitchen with a large peach crisp in one hand and a grocery bag in the other. "It's been too long!" She plopped the crisp on the counter and set the bag next to it, weaving around the bar stools to give Nicole a hug. "How can I help with dinner?"

"Nothing really, I think I'm done." Nicole returned the hug and surveyed the counter over Jessica's shoulder. Lasagna. Sliced bread. Salad. Dressings. Everything seemed to be in order.

Will and Hannah came running into the kitchen. "Mom, can I show Will the basement?"

"I think we're all going to head down there in a few minutes. Can you wait?"

Hannah wrinkled her nose. "I guess." She glanced at Will and grinned. "Have you seen the trailer for the new Spiderman?"

"Not yet."

Hannah looked at Nicole. "Can I show him on YouTube?"

"Sure, then come back and we can all head downstairs."

Jessica watched the two of them leave and moved the peach crisp closer to the basket of bread. "Hannah seems a little more relaxed since the last time I saw her. How's she adjusting to not competing this year?"

"Surprisingly well." Nicole fished a pair of salad tongs out of a drawer. "I think taking summer completely off was the best thing we could have done. She had more time with her friends and was able to dust off a few hobbies she'd forgotten about. She even helped with VBS."

"Ahh, yes. I was bummed to miss that this year," Jessica said. "It conflicted with our nephew's wedding in Idaho."

"It was a ton of fun. I hadn't done one of those for a while." Nicole stuck the tongs in the salad. "Anyway, when we told Hannah we wanted to keep dance down to twice a week with no competitions, she didn't seem to mind much. Plus, her dance teacher lets her help teach Abby's class and wants to give her a special solo in the Christmas recital, so that helps." Nicole dumped the remainder of a bag of croutons onto the salad and tossed it. "She actually mentioned hiring Hannah on when she's a little older."

"That's awesome." Jessica nodded to the grocery bag. "I brought ice cream. Can I stick it in your freezer?"

"Totally."

Jessica opened the drawer at the bottom of the fridge and jiggled the ice cream into place until it sat tucked between a bag of chicken and a box of corn dogs. "How are you adjusting to life with less dance?"

Nicole gave a dramatic sigh. "I *love* it." She grinned while Jessica laughed. "Seriously though, now that Hannah's schedule is more open and Kyle isn't doing football this year, my fall schedule feels like a dream." She waved her hand as she gestured to the kitchen. "I've cooked more in the past couple of months than I have in years because I'm actually home to do it."

Jessica looked concerned. "Is Kyle's leg okay?"

Nicole nodded. "Oh, he's fine. His doctor gave him the go-ahead for sports in the fall, but football has never been his favorite and he wanted to focus more on tech. He's trying to get an advanced robotics team started by Halloween." Jessica pulled out one of the bar stools and perched on top of it. Nicole slid a plate of crackers with goat cheese in front of her. "I made these as an appetizer, but I assume they'll be gone once the kids come in here so enjoy it now."

"Ooooo, nice." Jessica picked up a cracker and took a small scoop of cheese. "I take it Kyle liked Endeavor?"

"He loved it." Nicole gave a small laugh and shook her head. "We couldn't get him to stop talking about it for a solid week after he got back. It was probably the highlight of his summer, but only ask him about it if you're prepared to listen to a whole lot of geek-speak." She grabbed a stack of paper plates out of the pantry. "Tyler threatened to lock him in his room if he had to hear any more about coding."

Jessica chuckled. "Does Kyle like having him home? Permanently, I mean."

Nicole rolled her eyes and set the plates on the counter. "He'll say no if you ask him, but he absolutely does. They hang out more than either of them will admit." She let out a small laugh. "Looks like it won't be permanent though. One of the guys in his program has started going to Grace and the two of them are trying to find their own place after Christmas. But first, they need to find a couple of roommates so I'm soaking up having all of us home for a few more months."

"How does Tyler like working at Alliance Electric?"

"He likes it. He wishes he could work at Frontier with Sam, but they're not involved with the program through the college." Nicole headed back to the pantry for plastic cups. "Sam helped him pick out Alliance though. He has a couple of old coworkers who ended up there, and they have a good reputation."

"Does he miss Western?"

"Not even a little." Nicole snagged her own cracker. "Oh, remind me to tell you about the couple that moved in down the street. They're looking for a church, so I invited them to Grace." She smiled. "The mom mentioned to me that they've been feeling very overwhelmed now that their oldest has started school so I thought I might recommend the parenting class if they come—"

"What smells so good?" Tom's voice boomed as he and Sam made their way through to the kitchen. "Let me guess. Spaghetti? No, I see a casserole dish." He took a few steps toward the counter. "Lasagna! Even better."

Sam clapped a hand on Tom's shoulder. "She makes a mean one."

"I believe you." Tom pointed to the basement door. "Shall we?"

"I told the kids we'd all go down together," Nicole said. She wiped her hands on a towel and then on her jeans. "Hannah and Will should be back in a couple minutes."

Tom saw the plate of crackers and cheese and reached to help himself. "Sam was telling me he still has zero regrets on passing up that promotion." He popped a cracker into his mouth and winked. "I thought maybe he'd have second thoughts after selling his truck."

Nicole shook her head. "That was completely his idea. You can ask him. I was shocked."

Jessica looked from Nicole to Sam. "Wait, you sold your Ford?"

"And bought another—older—one," Sam said. "But this way we don't have a car payment."

Tom dipped another cracker in the cheese. "But you didn't have to sell it, right?"

"No." Nicole crossed her arms across her chest. "When he was offered the job, we spent a lot of time praying through it and sat down with the kids to discuss the pros and cons of Dad taking on a heftier position at work. Even though it was our call, we wanted their input." She shot a smile at Sam. "When Sam suggested we all look over our family vision and values together, I think it became clear pretty quickly the way we wanted to go."

Sam nodded. "I won't lie. It was tough on my pride."

"I bet," Tom said, his mouth full of cheese. "That job offered a lot."

"It did, but it also cost a lot of things we weren't willing to give up," Nicole said, remembering. March had been tense. Sam had felt pulled in two directions. A desire for the promotion contrasted with a drive to protect the relationships he'd been building in their family. Nicole had prayed more that month than she ever had in her life. She'd shared her concerns, listened to his dreams, and prayed that God would make it clear to Sam what was best. God had been kind, giving her a peace that surpassed understanding through it all, though the emotional baggage of waiting had her wondering more than once if she was developing a stomach ulcer.

Sam looked thoughtful. "The family vision was what sealed it for me. It made me realize that I'd be giving up a lot of what we'd been working toward." He slid an arm around Nicole. "We talked about it, and I decided I can always look into a position like that when the kids are older and out of the house. But for now, our time with them is limited, and I don't want to mess that up."

Tom nodded. "Is that also the reason you're golfing less these days? Jessica mentioned you're skipping Orlando this year."

"Yep. I'm doing the one for Christmas Cheer again, but I told the rest of my foursome I wanted a year off from the big trip."

Nicole leaned into Sam. "See? No regrets."

"And the truck didn't have anything to do with passing on the job," Sam said. "When I decided to stay in my current position, I realized that I could make some tweaks to some other areas that would benefit us financially in the long run. Just because I can afford a new truck doesn't mean I need one." He chuckled. "Though I do miss those heated seats."

"I miss those too," Kyle said, leading the way into the kitchen while the other teens trailed in behind him. "If you ever regret getting rid of that truck, it'll be at Christmas when we're all freezing our butts off."

Tyler elbowed him. "You can buy one when you're rich."

"Heck, no. I'm moving to Texas."

Tom clapped his hands together and jerked his head toward the basement door. "Shall we? I can't wait to see it all finished."

Sam grinned. "Lead the way."

Nicole waited until the rest of them had entered the stairwell before bringing up the rear. Sam's guess had been right: They had been fully functional by spring break, but the decor and finishing touches had come trickling in over the last few months. Their big family photo had arrived this week, making the basement officially complete. And she loved the final product.

"Oh, cool! You guys set up a family altar down here!" Whitney's voice floated up the stairs and Nicole smiled. They had all agreed that they wanted their family altar in the basement because it was where all of them naturally congregated. Sam had given Kyle permission to design the entire thing, and he'd done a beautiful job.

Nicole stepped onto the basement floor and stood back to admire the altar that was prominently displayed in the left corner of the family room. Kyle had designed it around a bookshelf that stood about four feet high, a large wooden cross hanging above it as the focal point. Battery-operated candles sat on a low candelabra on the top level, their lights flickering warmly over the polished wood. On the shelves themselves were family devotionals, small verse displays, a couple of photos, and several books. The bottom shelf held a handful of Bibles and a basket of family worship guides, alongside a stack of paper and a box of crayons.

"Kyle, this is amazing!" Whitney said, her eyes shining.

Kyle grinned sheepishly and ran a hand through his hair. "It was fun to design. I took some inspiration from the altar you guys have." He nodded at Sam. "And Dad helped me build the shelf."

"You built it?"

"Some of it."

Sam nudged Kyle. "Kyle did the vast majority of the work. I was mostly there to assist and offer advice."

Tom ran a hand over the wood. "It's gorgeous. Well done."

"Thanks."

Jessica turned away from the wall and her eyes fell upon the new canvas hanging on the wall behind the couch. "Your family photo finally came! I love it!"

Sam laughed. "I thought she'd pick one of the ones we took at Machu Picchu, but this one was her favorite." He flipped Nicole's hair. "Mine too, if I'm honest."

Tom studied the picture. "Where are you guys here?"

"I don't even remember the name of the village," Nicole said. "We were there for three days, and I kept getting it wrong, so I stopped trying."

Tyler smirked. "Should have taken Spanish, Mom."

Nicole shook her head at him. "When we're in Haiti next summer, you can thank me for studying French."

Tom looked at Sam in surprise. "You already have plans for next year?"

Sam nodded. "Going to Peru on a volunteer trip was by far our favorite family vacation we're ever taken. Yes?" He scanned the room as the rest of his family nodded at him. "We talked it over as soon as we got home and were all in agreement. We want to make this a regular thing." He winked at Abby. "Maybe every once in a while, we'll do Disney World or something, but we want to do these as often as possible."

Tom nodded in understanding. "One of the reasons you sold the truck?"

"For sure."

Jessica turned to Hannah. "How did you like Peru?"

Hannah bounced on the balls of her feet. "I liked it a lot. It was really different." She wrinkled her nose. "My phone didn't work very well."

Sam let out a barking laugh. "The great catastrophe of the trip."

Hannah made a good-natured face at her father. "It was okay, though. I mean, I still took pictures with it and stuff."

"I think Peru was a perfect first volunteer trip for us," Nicole said. "It was kind of a shock to the system, which was helpful. We were together the entire time and there weren't nearly as many distractions pulling at our attention when we were forced to be unplugged."

"How about you, Abby?" Tom directed his attention to their youngest.

"I really liked it," Abby said. "But I missed pizza."

Tom laughed. "I bet."

"You did a good job with the food," Nicole said. "And I'd brought some familiar snacks with us to have on hand when they gave us things that were a little too different. Our guide had recommended that, and I'm so glad I listened."

"A lot of the food was great though," Sam said. "I enjoyed most of it."

Tyler snorted. "Yeah, but I've never seen you so happy to eat McDonalds as you were when we were in Arequipa."

"Speaking of dinner," Sam said, waving his arm toward the stairs. "Should we head up? If that lasagna gets cold, it will be a tragedy."

The seven kids tromped up the stairs, with Tom and Jessica close behind them. Sam looked at Nicole, who hadn't moved. "You coming?"

"Go ahead and dish up, and I'll be there in time to pray."

"Sounds good."

Sam's footfalls died away at the top of the stairs and Nicole leaned her head against the wall. She could smell a hint of fresh paint. The carpet was still new enough to feel rich and soft, and she felt her lips turn up in a small smile.

Life was so different than it was a year ago. Maybe not noticeably to an outsider looking in, but in many ways their entire family had been transformed. Her table had rarely seen all six of them surrounding it in the last few years, but now everyone was home for dinner almost every night. She and Sam both faithfully read their Bibles and prayed as a couple. After-dinner family worship had become a regular part of their evening routine. They'd worked hard to get here, but the intentionality was seriously paying off.

Nicole's eyes strayed to the large canvas hanging over the couch. Sam was right. Usually she displayed the most perfect family photo she could find, like the one in the kitchen they'd taken last year in Mexico. Everyone smiling, everyone posing. Umbrella drinks and sunshine while the ocean sparkled in the background.

She much preferred this.

On the left, Abby was perched on top of Tyler's shoulders, a wide smile spread across her face as she all but strangled him in a hug beneath his chin. Tyler's arms were covered in mud up to his elbows, and he held a dirty water bottle in one hand. His smile was as wide as Abby's. On the right stood Kyle, arms equally dirty, as he and Tyler were halfway through building a mud stove in one of the villager's houses. He had an arm around Hannah and was blowing a raspberry at her. Hannah was mid-giggle, her arms full of art supplies because she had been snagged for the photo on her way to draw with some of the local children.

She and Sam stood in the center, a smudge of mud on Sam's left cheek. He had a toolbox in one hand and his other arm around Nicole. Nicole's shorts were filthy, and her hair was thrown up in a messy bun, but she was beaming. Sam's head was thrown back in a giant laugh.

The trip had been a dream. Not in the shiny, sparkly way a resort vacation could be, but in the goodness and joy it had provided. They had spent ten full days in Peru. Hot. Sweaty. Surrounded by bugs. They'd missed a connecting flight and had to improvise. They'd struggled through more than one rough night of sleep. But they'd also spent ten days *together*. Working side-by-side. No distractions. Helping others. Trying new foods and eating meal after meal as a family. They'd even gotten to go sight-seeing for two days and explored Macchu Picchu and a gorgeous natural hot spring.

Nicole watched the candle lights flicker as she flipped the switch at the base of the stairs, plunging the basement into dimness. Laughter floated down to her ears, and she climbed toward the kitchen.

Things weren't perfect. Things would never be perfect. But there was one crucial difference between their family last year and their family now: God was at the center. Not just in word, but in deed.

Nicole ran a finger along the railing as she slowly made her way up the stairs.

Life was different.

They were different.

And different was good.

LESSON SUMMARY:

Now that you've read about one family's parenting journey, you may want to review the lessons they learned. Here is a brief overview of the steps outlined in this book. The lessons can be remembered by the **Faithful Parent Proven Process** and the acronym **STEWARD**.

FAITHFUL PARENT PROVEN PROCESS

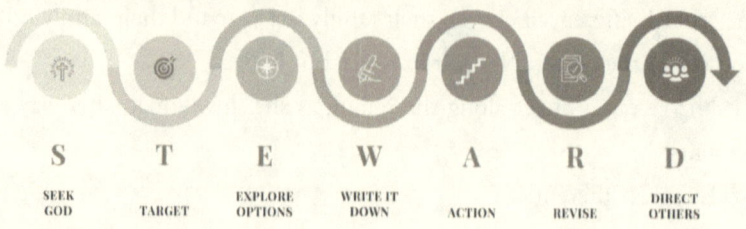

S	T	E	W	A	R	D
SEEK GOD	TARGET	EXPLORE OPTIONS	WRITE IT DOWN	ACTION	REVISE	DIRECT OTHERS

Seek God – Learn to be more A.D.E.P.T. (Attentive, Discipline, Encourage, Provide, Teach) parents as you spend more time in God's word individually and as a family.

Target/Trajectory - Clarify the vision and values of your Christian family to help ensure you are all walking together on your family journey.

Explore Options - There are many ways to parent. Take time to explore options that might be more consistent with your Christian family vision and values.

Write it Down - Take time to put into words and write down a parenting plan that will keep your family focused on your journey.

Action - Learn how to successfully implement your plan.

Review and Revise - Incorporate ways to review your plan and progress on a regular basis and make changes to that plan as needed.

Direct Others - When your family is on a clear and focused path, you will be blessed and also be a blessing to others by helping other families who may be struggling on their Christian family journey.

For more resources on how to use this plan in your family, go to our website faithfulparent.org.

The steps outlined in this book are also part of our Faithful Parent Academy, our online course that will help you: create your family's personalized family vision statement; clarify and write your family values; create a unique parenting plan; implement your plan and start seeing changes quickly.

Go to https://www.faithfulparent.org/academy to learn more about our Faithful Parent Academy.

Thank you for purchasing and taking the time to read *A Chance to Change*. We are so thankful and hope you found value in it. Please consider sharing it with friends and family and also leaving a review online. Your feedback and support are always appreciated.

How can I apply these lessons to my family?

Are you ready to stop experiencing the stress, busyness, and chaos that comes with your normal family routine and start living a more fun, focused, connected family life that is closer to God?

Get the tools, resources, direction, and time that you need to develop a clear parenting plan specific for your family based on your vision and values.

To learn more about Faithful Parent please visit the following: www.faithfulparent.org

Facebook: https://www.facebook.com/FaithfulParent

Instagram: @faithfulparentmom

ABOUT THE AUTHORS

Derek and Amy Weichel are a husband and wife writing team who were both born and raised in the rural Midwest. Derek graduated from medical school and completed a residency program in orthopaedic surgery. Amy went into teaching. Now the two are happily living with their family in Nebraska where Derek works as an orthopaedic surgeon at the local community hospital and Amy homeschools their 4 children, Cole, Leah, Lexi, and Lily.

As part of their desire to create the right environment and surroundings in which to raise their children, Derek and Amy were led to write this book. They have used the process outlined in it to create their own intentional parenting plan that has transformed how they raise their children in all aspects, especially in their intentional teaching of God's word in the home.

In addition, they also founded Faithful Parent, a ministry that is dedicated to providing help to parents, including free guides, blog posts, courses, and even photographs of their many foreign adventures.

In their free time, Derek and Amy, along with their children, enjoy traveling and have enjoyed some amazing vacations to some special places, including 6 international volunteer trips as a family to Peru, Costa Rica, South Africa, Kenya, Guatemala and Indonesia. Both Derek and Amy are lifelong learners who enjoy reading and learning individually and together as a couple.

As far as the future is concerned, Derek and Amy want to continue to provide resources that help parents develop a Christian parenting plan which will keep their families intentionally focused on Jesus for this generation and future generations.

You can contact, follow or connect with Derek and Amy Weichel at:

Blog: https://www.faithfulparent.org

Facebook: https://www.facebook.com/FaithfulParent

Instagram: @faithfulparentmom

Email: amy@faithfulparent.org

www.ingramcontent.com/pod-product-compliance
Lightning Source LLC
Chambersburg PA
CBHW022142240626
47153CB00007B/2470